It couldn't be him, but it was.

She was first struck by how tall he'd grown, that she found herself looking up to him.

Cole was a man now, strong shouldered and lean. Her breath caught as heat twisted through her blood. Dread pulsed in her throat.

"I don't know what the hell you're doing here, Cole," she said, her voice strong even while her legs felt weak. "But you can go pack your things. You're not welcome."

The tension hung thick in the air, and just looking at him made her feel small and panicked. No matter what had changed, no matter how many years had passed, Cole Dempsey represented a moment in time she'd give anything to erase.

"I'm not going anywhere, Bryn," he said, breaking the stony silence. "And you can't make me."

Dear Reader,

Let April shower you with the most thrilling romances around—from Silhouette Intimate Moments, of course. We love Karen Templeton's engaging characters and page-turning prose. In her latest story, *Swept Away* (#1357), from her miniseries THE MEN OF MAYES COUNTY, a big-city heroine goes on a road trip and gets stranded in tiny Haven, Oklahoma…with a very handsome cowboy and his six kids. Can this rollicking group become a family? *New York Times* bestselling author Ana Leigh returns with another BISHOP'S HEROES romance, *Reconcilable Differences* (#1358), in which two lovers reunite as they play a deadly game to fight international terror.

You will love the action and heavy emotion of *Midnight Hero* (#1359) in Diana Duncan's new FOREVER IN A DAY miniseries. Here, a SWAT cop has to convince his sweetheart to marry him—while trying to survive a hostage situation! And get ready for Suzanne McMinn to take you by storm in *Cole Dempsey's Back in Town* (#1360), in which a rakish hero must clear his name and face the woman he's never forgotten.

Catch feverish passion and high stakes in Nina Bruhns's *Blue Jeans and a Badge* (#1361). This tale features a female bounty hunter who arrests a very exasperating—very sexy— chief of police! Can these two get along long enough to catch a dangerous criminal? And please join me in welcoming new author Beth Cornelison to the line. In *To Love, Honor and Defend* (#1362), a tormented beauty enters a marriage of convenience with an old flame…and hopes that he'll keep her safe from a stalker. Will their relationship deepen into true love? Don't miss this touching and gripping romance!

So, sit back, prop up your feet and enjoy the ride with Silhouette Intimate Moments. And be sure to join us next month for another stellar lineup.

Happy reading!

Patience Smith
Associate Senior Editor

Please address questions and book requests to:
Silhouette Reader Service
U.S.: 3010 Walden Ave., P.O. Box 1325, Buffalo, NY 14269
Canadian: P.O. Box 609, Fort Erie, Ont. L2A 5X3

Cole Dempsey's Back in Town

SUZANNE McMINN

Silhouette®

INTIMATE MOMENTS™

Published by Silhouette Books

America's Publisher of Contemporary Romance

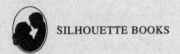

SILHOUETTE BOOKS

ISBN 0-373-27430-0

COLE DEMPSEY'S BACK IN TOWN

Visit Silhouette Books at www.eHarlequin.com

Printed in U.S.A.

SUZANNE McMINN

lives by a lake in North Carolina with her husband and three kids, plus a bunch of dogs, cats and ducks. Visit her Web site at www.SuzanneMcMinn.com to learn more about her books, newsletter and contests. Check out www.paxleague.com for news, info and fun bonus features connected to her "PAX League" series about paranormal superagents!

With much love to my husband, Gerald, who is always there for me.

Chapter 1

The house looked the same.

Minus the dead body, of course.

Cole Dempsey stared up the oak-canopied drive to the classic columns fronting the antebellum Bellefleur Plantation. The Greek revival-style monstrosity had filled his waking fantasies and sleeping nightmares for fifteen long and bitter years. Someone owed. He was here to collect.

Look out, Azalea Bend, Louisiana. Cole Dempsey had returned. And this time, he had something to back up his claims.

He left his black Cobra at the head of the drive, preferring to walk to the door, overnight case in hand. He

needed the time and space to take it in, to comprehend
that the house was no haunted vision; it was real. The
mansion rose before him as timeless as the Mississippi that flowed behind it, holding its secrets, its lies,
its fears, its ghosts. And sweet, false Bryn Louvel.

Now that he was here, the emotions that came with
the magnolia-laden air, the river-swept breeze, the
memory-churned past hit harder than he'd expected.
Amidst the buzzes, hums and whispers of the late-
spring evening came the sounds of the past—the men-
tal audio reel of another May night. The scream that
no one in the whole of St. Salome Parish would forget, the thundering footsteps, the shouts in the thick
night, the wailing of a mother…and the terrible ac-
cusation that had ended in a ringing shot.

The lights of the columned portico drew him.

He had been promised the corner bedroom on the
second floor, overlooking the river. The Oleander
Room, as he had been told it was now called, boasted
a rosewood half-tester double bed and a private verandah. All the rooms included decanters of refresh-
ment beverages, a guided mansion tour and a wake-up
call with hot coffee, juice and sweet potato muffins
as well as a full plantation breakfast.

As if he gave a damn about any of that.

Cole took the massive steps of the columned portico in athletic strides. Lifting the ornate brass
knocker, he pounded it forcefully against the heavy
door in the center of the portico. Up close, he noticed

the peeling paint on the sides of the building. The surrounding gardens, what he could see of them in the spill of the porch light, were overgrown. The eighteenth-century-era mansion had survived colonial and civil wars and the perils of time, but it appeared that murder had brought it to its knees.

Open to the public for tours weekdays from 9:00 a.m. to 4:00 p.m. announced the small lettered plaque in the center of the door. How that would have galled Bryn's father.

The sound of footsteps near the door elicited an answering jerk in his pulse. He needed Bryn. He couldn't get to the truth without her help.

But instead of Bryn, the woman who greeted him was young, maybe twenty, with a pixie-fresh face, curly strawberry-blond hair and bright eyes that held no shadows.

"Welcome to Bellefleur!" The young woman made a gesture inviting Cole into the majestic chandelier-lit foyer. Her voice was bubbly, her movements energetic.

A sweeping, free-standing staircase carved from walnut rose at the back of the large entry area, flanked by floor-to-ceiling oil paintings of a long-ago master and mistress of Bellefleur. Wide-arched openings led to huge rooms. Cole knew one was the parlor, the other a library, all furnished in period style.

"I'm Melodie Ladd. You must be Mr. Granville." Shutting the door, the young woman moved past him to station herself behind a rococo table in the center of the foyer.

A guest book lay open and she held out a fountain pen. Cole set down his case.

"Actually, it's Dempsey, Cole Dempsey," he said, and watched her face. There was no reaction. "I'm with *the* Granville, Piers and Rousseau. There must have been a misunderstanding when my secretary made the reservation." He smiled his charming smile.

There was, of course, no misunderstanding. Never forewarn the enemy. He had learned that and more in law school.

"Oh! Well, Mr. Dempsey, then." The young woman waited as he signed the book, then launched into a perky speech. "We're so glad you've chosen the Bellefleur Bed and Breakfast for your stay in Plantation Country. We specialize in escape from the three T's—telephones, television and traffic. If you have a need to use a telephone, there is one available in the plantation office. Also, we'll be happy to assist in arrangements to take advantage of any of the area attractions—"

Cole cut her off. "I'm here to work."

"I see." She carried on, "There is a coffeemaker, microwave and small refrigerator in each room. Check-out is 11:00 a.m. on your day of departure— let's see, I have you down for two weeks, is that right?" She consulted a ledger.

"I may need to stay longer, if the room is available."

She looked surprised, but quickly nodded. "That would be wonderful! I'll let Miss Louvel know. We've only recently opened, so we aren't booked up. In fact, you're our only guest tonight."

That was what Cole's research had led him to believe. Turning the plantation into a bed and breakfast was a last-ditch effort to prevent seizure. Property taxes were a bitch, especially when you got behind. Even as Cole's star had risen, the Louvels' had fallen on hard times.

But there would be no sympathy in Cole's dead, ruined heart for anyone in Azalea Bend, much less a Louvel. After all, they had shown none to him or his family.

"I'll show you to your room," Melodie offered, gesturing toward the grand staircase that wound up three stories from the foyer. "If you'd like, you may take advantage of the refreshments waiting there or take a stroll down to the river. Tomorrow, if you like, I can escort you on a guided tour of the mansion."

"I'd like Miss Louvel to take me on the tour."

A look of sudden caution crossed Melodie's face.

"She's the owner of the house, isn't she?" he explained. "I'd simply prefer she be the one to tell me about its history. I can wait till she's available."

"Yes, she owns the house, Mr. Dempsey." Melodie gave him another long look, and for a second he thought—

Dempsey.

Did the name mean anything to her? Even at her age, she would have heard the stories.

"I'm sure Miss Louvel will be happy to show you around the mansion tomorrow," Melodie said finally. "Shall we go up then?" She led the way upstairs.

The room was everything it was advertised to be. Spacious, clean, stripped of any reminder that the brutally murdered Aimee Louvel had once slept there.

"Please, make yourself at home at Bellefleur," Melodie said, exiting the room. There was a pitcher of ice water along with a decanter of merlot, and a spread of crackers, sliced cheeses and fruit on the low table in the sitting area. He turned over a crystal glass and poured the merlot.

He took the wine with him when he went back down the stairs and through the lonely, low-lit parlor, to the dark dining room, then beyond, to the wide back porch that spanned the rear of the mansion. He leaned against the columned edge and gazed out toward the shadowed thickness that he knew was trees and river.

A slow sip of merlot later, he closed his eyes, let the unstoppable past roll over him. He wondered, not for the first time, what Bryn was like all these years later. She would be thirty-one years old and…beautiful. Surely she was beautiful. She and her twin Aimee had been fairy princesses in a tower. Rich, sheltered and spoiled. Two perfect golden-haired fairies with their purple hyacinth eyes. He remembered the last time he'd known hope, he'd stood in this spot, holding sweet-sixteen Bryn's hand—

When he opened his eyes and turned back toward the house, she was there.

It couldn't be him, but it was.

He leaned against the white pillar of the porch, wineglass in hand, and watched her with that steely will of his that she remembered all too well. He straightened, as casually as if this were his home and not hers. The shadows melted away and the ghost of the past was replaced by the reality of the present as he walked into the light.

She was struck first by how tall he'd grown; she found herself looking up to him. Cole Dempsey was a man now, dark-haired, strong-shouldered and lean. Unable to stop herself, she thought of the nights they'd shared together, exploring each other's bodies. Experiencing the joy and passion of first love. Her breath caught as heat twisted through her blood. Dread pulsed in her throat.

Bryn Louvel hated herself for it, but she took a step back and struggled to control the havoc his reappearance had wrought in her emotions.

"I don't know what the hell you're doing here, Cole, what kind of trick you think you're pulling," she said, her voice strong even while her legs felt weak. "But you can go pack your things. You're not welcome at Bellefleur."

The tension hung thick in the air for a long beat before he spoke, and just looking at him made her feel suffocated and small and panicked. No matter what had changed, no matter how many years had passed, Cole Dempsey represented a moment in time she'd give anything to erase. Her first love had been destroyed as surely as her sister.

She couldn't look at Cole without thinking of his father and everything that had happened the awful night that had changed everything.

"I'm not going anywhere, Bryn," he said, breaking the stony silence. "And you can't make me." He took another step toward her, as if he meant to close in on her by slow degrees. He set his glass down on a nearby wrought-iron table.

"That sounds very mature, Cole. I can see you've grown up."

"*You* certainly have," he responded. His eyes took her in, boldly swept her from head to toe. "Bryn Louvel, all grown up."

Though her traitorous body tingled from his thorough appraisal, she spoke stiffly. "That's right. I've grown up. This is my home and I'd like you to leave."

Still he came towards her. "Ah, this may be your home, Bryn, but it's also your business. I've paid for the right to stay here. How things change. Once my father was paid to work at Bellefleur. Now I'm the one paying you. Ironic, don't you think?"

She refused to answer his taunt. "Don't mention your father in this house," she said instead.

Cole stood in front of her now, his proximity overwhelming. "What about *your* father, Bryn?" he demanded softly, too close. "What if I mention him?"

"He's dead. They're all dead. Your father, mine, Aimee. It's all over, Cole. So leave." Her voice rose. "Get out of my house."

"But it's not over, not yet," he countered calmly, as if they were discussing the news instead of the fifteen-year-old crime that had destroyed both their families. "Do you know that Aimee's death is the oldest unsolved murder in St. Salome Parish?"

"It's not an unsolved murder."

"Oh yes, it is." He came at her now with furious speed, and when she backed up again, she stumbled against a potted bougainvillea. He grabbed her shoulders, bare in her sleeveless blouse, and steadied her. "But I'm here to solve it. And you're going to help me."

She braced her hands against his chest and pushed him away. "Let go of me, Cole." And he did, but the chilling heat of his touch on her skin remained, as did the haunting threat of his words. He scared her, and that thought was shocking. She had never been frightened of him before.

Fifteen years ago, she'd loved him. It was the first and only time in her life she'd ever given her heart away so completely. Even now, she knew there was a part of her that she held back from any man she'd become close to since.

Whether any future relationship could overcome what had happened fifteen years ago, she didn't know yet. And Cole had been part of that horror. He belonged to another lifetime, and he had no place in her here and now. He was not that tender boy she had once loved any more than she was that naive sixteen-year-old girl. At thirty-two, his face had taken on a mature seasoning that was both handsome and cold. And his eyes, oh God, they were the worst. She would have known them anywhere, and yet it was as if she'd never looked into them before. Gold flecks like solar flares dotted in the brilliant green of them, compelling and yet bitter now, the gentleness all gone.

Cole Dempsey the man was hard as stone.

"If you're here to dig up the past, the last thing I'll ever do is help you," she promised. "So if that's what you're here for, you're wasting your time. There are several perfectly fine new motels closer to town—"

He shook his head. "You're running a business here, Bryn. What kind of business turns away customers? Especially a business that's in dire need of cash flow."

She carefully schooled her features to reveal nothing of the clean shot he'd achieved. Yes, Bellefleur was in trouble. When the sugar mill had gone under, they'd nearly lost everything. Her father's drinking and gambling had consumed the last years of his life.

Maurice Louvel had drowned himself in alcohol and debts until he couldn't see his way to the surface anymore, then he'd shot himself by the edge of the reflecting pond.

"Your father ruined us," she bit out. "He got the revenge he'd sworn, didn't he? He killed Aimee and destroyed my father—"

"And your father did nothing?"

His gaze bored into her.

"*Your* father deserved everything that happened to him," Bryn hissed back. "For what he did to Aimee. How dare you ask me to care what happened to him after that? Do you think it was easy for my family?"

Her nightmares about that night were both surreal and vivid. Over and over, she had to hear her sister's scream, her mother's cries in the darkness, her father's frantic running, lights flashing over the grounds, and the angry shouts, a popping gunshot and the silence. The silence was the most horrible part.

In the silence, she always saw Aimee, face up at the edge of the reflecting pool, bloody, battered, her life gone. And Wade Dempsey beside her at the pond's bank, one bullet clean through his heart, gazing lifelessly up at the death-dark sky. A bullet Maurice Louvel had fired.

Ten years later, Bryn's father had placed himself in that same spot, only this time he'd shot himself. He'd won his freedom in a courtroom, but he could never forgive himself for inspiring the revenge that had made Wade Dempsey kill Aimee. To the end, her father had blamed himself for his daughter's murder.

Cole's voice was as bitter as the look in his eyes. "Oh, I hope it was hard, Bryn. I hope it was very hard. Your father was judge, jury and executioner that night."

"He was out of his mind that night. Who wouldn't be after finding their daughter dead in their own backyard?"

"Oh, I know all about it. Temporary insanity. He got off, didn't he? No court in St. Salome Parish would convict a war hero and the town's biggest employer, would they? Even if it was all lies. That's right." He kept his agonizing gaze on her. "Lies. Do you know I've read every document I could get my hands on connected to your sister's murder, Bryn? Have you?"

"No," she said finally. She couldn't bear it. She didn't want to know more about that night than she already did. The bitter strife between her parents, the near-violent altercation when her father had fired Wade Dempsey, and the horror of everything that followed. It was enough. Too much.

Bryn would never forget the betrayed fire in Cole's eyes when she'd sat across a courtroom from him months later when the verdict was read and Maurice Louvel was acquitted for taking a father's justice. But she had lost Cole even before that last day of the trial, and there was no going back. She'd had to start over, just as he and his mother had had to do when they had left Azalea Bend. Her father hadn't been able to start over, though.

Her father had lost more than a daughter that night. He'd lost his will to work and even to live. His business had been destroyed, his family broken. Battered beyond repair, just like Aimee.

Nothing had ever been the same.

"Your father lied," Cole said. "Your mother lied. And you lied, Bryn. And we both know it."

Guilt was a horrible thing, but Bryn had learned to live with it. The only lie she'd told wouldn't change the fact that Wade Dempsey had murdered Aimee. Her father's pride, her mother's dignity—it was little enough to leave them after they'd lost Aimee.

And for that, to save what was left of her family, Bryn had lied. To Cole, it had been betrayal. To Bryn, it had been her only choice for her family's survival.

"Go away, Cole. If you can't let go of the past, that's your problem."

"Oh no, that's where you're wrong. It's your problem, too—because you and your family weren't the only ones who lied. This whole town is full of liars, and I might not have been able to prove that fifteen years ago, but things are different now."

Bryn's blood ran cold. Oh, this wasn't the first time she'd heard Cole's conspiracy theory about the prosecution. Even at seventeen, he'd been determined that his father had been innocent. But he wasn't seventeen anymore.

What havoc could Cole's misplaced, bitter loyalty create now? He blamed an entire town for his father's downfall. And she knew he also blamed her. She'd hurt him, she knew that. But he'd also hurt her more than he could possibly realize. She'd never imagined she could be as close to anyone as she was to Aimee—until she'd fallen in love with Cole. Then she'd lost them both in one night.

And he could still hurt her. She had a business to build, and everything depended on its success.

"Aimee's murder is the last thing I plan to discuss with you, Cole." She gave her words the ring of finality, but she might as well have flung them at a stone wall for all the effect they appeared to have on Cole.

"It's late, and I realize seeing me again is…upsetting," he said. "We'll talk tomorrow."

God, he was arrogant. "I'm not upset, Cole. I'm not bound by the past as you clearly are." She took another step back, bumping into the column behind her.

"Did you know I'm an attorney now?" he went on in his quiet-steel voice as if she'd said nothing. The lethal ice of his eyes prickled uneasiness up the nape of her neck. "That's right. I worked my way through college, made something of myself that no one in Azalea Bend thought possible. Especially you, isn't that right, Bryn?"

He stood a breath away, and with the column

pressed against her back, she had no room to get away. She was trapped, in every way possible.

"You're looking at the newest partner in Granville, Piers and Rousseau. That's the biggest law firm in Baton Rouge, if you don't know," he continued, lifting his hand and running the tips of his fingers down the side of her face. Her pulse jumped in response. "I'm a man now, Bryn. Not a boy. I won't be tucking my tail between my legs and running away this time. And I won't be a victim to the Louvels any longer. I'm going to finish this, once and for all."

The marsh grasses down by the river shuddered in the long beat. Bryn felt her heart sink inside her. He might be wearing a plain polo shirt, both buttons undone, and laid-back jeans, but his looks were deceptively simple. His bearing alone revealed the truth of who he had become even if she hadn't seen the sleek new sports car in the drive. Cole Dempsey was a success, but the question of what drove him was what really unnerved her.

He was a man on a mission. But was it justice…or revenge?

Chapter 2

She wished she hadn't sent Melodie home.

The main house of Bellefleur was over nine thousand square feet, but with no one else in the mansion tonight but Cole Dempsey, it felt about the size of an airplane lavatory.

Bryn hugged her knees up to her chest, sitting in the middle of the mahogany four-poster in the main second floor bedroom. She had her own private sitting area and a small personal office. It had been her parents' suite, which Bryn had made over for herself. In the years following Aimee's death, her mother had spent more time in than out of hospitals being treated for depression. Patsy Louvel had finally come back to Bellefleur—but only to one of the cottages on the grounds, self-imprisoned with her beloved camellias, her keening grief and later, a full-time nurse.

Sometimes Bryn thought she hated Bellefleur as much she loved it, but all she knew for sure was that after more than two hundred years she couldn't be the Louvel who let it go. She had plans, lots of them. Other families along Louisiana's famed River Road, Highway 18, that traversed the state following the path of the mighty Mississippi, had found ways to keep their plantations. They offered overnight accommodations, tours, Old South history and craft events.

Slowly, she would be able to finance restoration work on the house and grounds to bring them back to their former glory. Her father's pride and outdated sense of Louvel nobility would never have allowed it, but now that he was gone, Bryn had taken over. After high school, she'd learned the historic tourism business from the ground up, working for several of the most successful historic plantations as everything from receptionist to tour guide and finally manager. It hadn't left her with much time for relationships, but she hadn't cared. Saving Bellefleur had been her goal.

She was starting small, with only herself, Melodie, who worked part-time while finishing college, and the few additional employees she could afford, but the possibilities were endless.

She was even in the process of convincing a Cre-

ole chef who had once cooked for her parents to create a restaurant at Bellefleur—if she could get the financial backing. First she had to prove to the bank that
she could make a success of the bed and breakfast
she'd already opened.

Now Cole Dempsey threatened everything.

He'd returned to unearth a scandal just when she
was trying to turn Bellefleur into a tourist destination.
She didn't need talk of murder darkening her chances.
Especially if Cole was determined that it was an *unsolved* murder. That meant the real murderer was still
out there, possibly even near Bellefleur. Which
couldn't be true, but what would the mere rumor do
to her business?

The soothing palette of ivory, oatmeal and gray in
the grand bedroom suite that had once been her parents wasn't soothing tonight. Bryn rose, paced to the
verandah doors, pushing back the creamy silk drapes
outlined with grosgrain ribbon. She stared out at the
thick, unknowable night. He'd booked two weeks already and had asked Melodie if he could stay longer.
And what was worse, seeing him *had* upset her. Damn
him for knowing it so easily, too.

She was still in shock from seeing him, in fact. His
chiseled, hard face was almost unrecognizable as that
young, gentle teen who'd wooed her in the summer
gardens long ago. He'd slip up from the sugarcane
fields to find her, his bare muscular arms glistening
in the humid heat. He would wink at her, watch her

with his remarkable eyes, cast her smiles, and slowly, with his whispered words and stolen kisses, he drew her into his magic world of hopes and dreams. He'd always wanted to make something of himself. He'd been ambitious and arrogant even then.

And she, who had known nothing but privilege, was awed by him. In those days, she'd had everything but feared her own shadow. He'd had nothing but exuded the confidence that he could do anything. Together, they'd steal away on secret dates, sometimes with Aimee's help, and other times without it—like the night he'd tempted her down the latticed ivywork outside her window and made love to her for the first time under the star-splashed sky.

He'd made her believe that, like him, she could do anything, too. But the truth had been that neither of them could control the events that had torn them apart.

Damn him for coming back.

The phone in her office rang. Bryn hurried across the aged heart-pine floor, her bare feet padding silently. While none of the visitor accommodations included telephones for the sake of their guests' serenity during their stay, Bryn kept phones installed in her personal office here as well as her business office downstairs. They were the only two land lines in the main house.

"Just checking to see how your meeting went with the bank today," came Drake Cavanaugh's voice in response to her hello.

Bryn hesitated, despite the fact he was her oldest friend and had stood by her ever since Aimee's death. Their relationship had grown by gentle degrees from friendship to fondness, and only recently had Drake expressed a desire to take their longstanding relationship to the next level. His marriage proposal had taken her completely by surprise, though looking back, she realized she'd ignored the signs of his changing feelings.

And now that Cole was back, she knew why.

She'd walled up her emotions fifteen years ago. She'd loved Cole with her whole heart, and the day he'd broken it it had nearly killed her. She'd been protecting herself ever since. Even with Drake.

"It went fine," she said finally. "But I need to have a good year, that's all. Then we'll take a look at the books and they'll decide if I'm ready for a loan."

"I'd co-sign and you could get a loan now."

"I know." Bryn cradled the phone against her shoulder as she slipped into the comfortable wingback chair behind her desk. "But you know I won't do that." Especially now that Drake had revealed his deeper feelings for her. She couldn't let herself become indebted to him that way, not if she wasn't sure she would marry him.

"You know I'll keep offering," he said. Bryn was quiet, and after a beat, Drake asked, "Is something wrong?"

There was no point in keeping it a secret. Melodie

was a chatterbox. The whole town would know by tomorrow. As soon as Melodie mentioned the name of their new guest, people would recognize it. Melodie was young, but even she had heard the story, if not the name of Wade Dempsey's son. Dempsey itself was a common enough surname, but plenty of older residents in Azalea Bend would remember and put it together.

"Cole Dempsey's back in town."

"You're kidding."

Now Drake was quiet.

"I wish I were. He's staying here. He booked a room."

Drake let out a curse beneath his breath.

"He's a lawyer now. In Baton Rouge. Have you heard of Granville, Piers and Rousseau?"

"He's in with them?" Bryn could hear the shock in Drake's voice.

"Yes. Or, he said he was."

"Do you want me to come over? I'm in the city tonight, but—"

"I'm fine." As a member of the state congress, Drake spent a lot of time in Baton Rouge, had a lot of connections. He kept his parents' old Georgian in Azalea Bend for his frequent visits to St. Salome Parish. "Maybe you could check out his story. Find out if he's really with the Granville, Piers and Rousseau firm."

She didn't really doubt Cole on that fact, but it

seemed wise to check. She couldn't think of anything else to do and she was grasping at straws. She promised Drake she would call if Cole caused trouble, but she knew she wouldn't. Drake and Cole had never been friends, and she doubted the passage of time had lessened that tension. As the prosecutor for St. Salome Parish, Drake's father had handled—or deliberately mishandled, according to Cole—the case against Maurice Louvel, leading to his acquittal for the shooting of Wade Dempsey. Once, years ago, she had confided in Drake about her secret affair with Cole. And the fact that now Drake had let her know about his true feelings for her could only make things worse. She was about to go back to bed when the phone chirped again.

"Bryn, it's Melodie. I stopped by the Kwik Pak on the way home and ran into Mr. Brouchard. I mentioned Cole Dempsey and he told me who he was. Why didn't you tell me Cole Dempsey was Wade Dempsey's son? I'm so sorry! I feel awful about just leaving you there."

"It's all right. It's no big deal." Maybe if Bryn kept telling people that Cole Dempsey being back in town was no big deal, no one would pay any attention to him. *Spin control.*

"Do you want me to come back?" Melodie asked. "I could get my things, spend the night."

"No. I'm fine. Thanks, anyway. You have class in the morning. You don't need to be way out here." Melodie attended college part-time in Baton Rouge.

"He's— Well, he's not like I expected," Melodie said.

"What did you expect?" He was everything Bryn had expected and worse.

"I don't know. He's so— Gorgeous. Charming. Rich. My God, did you see that Cobra in the drive? I just didn't expect—I guess I had in mind this hired hand's son, a kid from the wrong side of the tracks, a bad boy."

"People change," Bryn said briefly. "Thanks for calling, Melodie, but I'm all right."

She hung up. The linen-upholstered walls with their hand-stenciled white medallions seemed to close in on her. She tried to sleep, but only tossed and turned. The room felt suffocating, and her mind wouldn't stop turning. She got up, pulled off her pajamas and put on shorts and a pink hibiscus-colored T-shirt. Silently, she slipped into the hall, padded barefoot down the main stairs—

And slammed straight into a hard shadow at the bottom of the steps. Strong arms grabbed her, held her tight. He smelled like musk and man, and a hopeless need built inside of her.

"Dammit, Bryn, you'll kill yourself barreling down stairs in the dark like that," Cole said.

"And you would care."

She shook him off, trying to ignore the effect his hands had on her body. Her pulse jumped off the scale and she felt as if her heart was in her throat. It was bad enough that he was back—the last thing she could handle was him touching her.

"What are you doing wandering around the house in the night?" she demanded, as if she weren't doing the same thing.

"I went for a walk down by the river."

Was he restless, too? Why? She wanted—and didn't want—to know what he was thinking.

"What are *you* doing wandering around in the night?" he asked in turn.

She said nothing. In the spectral dark she could see the bright shine of his eyes and something deep inside her quivered when he reached back up and touched her cheek.

"I don't want to hurt you, Bryn," he said in a quiet voice. "That's not why I came to you."

For some strange reason, the tenderness of his words made her want to cry.

"Then why did you come?" she whispered tautly.

In the teeming silence, she saw something in his eyes shift, heat, and there it was, the inexplicable seductive frisson tugging her toward him just as it had on those long-ago days in the summer shadows of Bellefleur. And she understood why she was suddenly struggling to contain tears. But before he could speak, the screech of a tire from outside pulled her away, then the sound of shattering glass broke the night.

Chapter 3

Something crashed on the floor of the front hall mere feet away, and there was another screeching sound. Bryn's stomach dipped crazily. She froze for just an instant, her brain computing facts. That sound was a car, and that crash was something thrown through the window. She pushed past the hard shadow of Cole. Her bare feet raced across the wood floor and she flung open the door even as she registered the stab of something sharp and ice-hot.

"Wait, Bryn!" Cole came up behind her, grabbed her as she would have torn outside onto the portico. The half moon that had lit the grounds earlier in the evening hid behind clouds, and beyond the splash of

the porch lantern, she could see nothing but imper-
meable dark.

"Let go of me," she demanded, fighting Cole's too-
intimate arms plastering her to his too-hard body.

"They're gone." He relaxed his hold.

Bryn hit the switch in the entry hall. The overhead
chandelier spilled blinding light down on the room.
Her breath jammed her throat.

Glass lay everywhere. A rust-red brick sat inno-
cently amongst the shards. It took a beat for her to register the fact that something was tied to it.

She took a step toward it and cried out in pain.

"Bryn!" Cole reached out to her again. As his arms
went around her, he felt her trembling.

He knew the last thing she wanted was his help.
"I'm fine," she said.

"You're hurt."

"There's a note." She started to hobble her way
across the glass-littered pine floor, but Cole—wearing
shoes—crunched straight for the brick and reached it
before her. He knelt and picked it up. A small sheet of
white paper was tied to it with a strand of twine.

He ripped it off and opened it. The block-lettered
words burned up at him.

The son of a murderer isn't welcome in St.
Salome Parish.

The old bitter fury washed through him, thick and
greasy and nauseating.

"What does it say?"

He stood, turned. Bryn's face was pale, anxious. She was good and freaked-out by what had just happened, and he tamped down his own rage against the past and this town and the injustice he'd waited fifteen years to make right. He handed her the note.

She read it and lifted huge, haunted eyes to him. The small piece of paper shook in her slender fingers. "We have to call the police," she said hoarsely.

"Right. That'll help." He couldn't stop the sarcasm that laced his words. The police in St. Salome Parish hadn't given a rat's ass about the Dempseys fifteen years ago and he wouldn't be surprised if that hadn't changed. The Dempseys' nomadic lifestyle, moving from sugarcane plantation to sugarcane plantation every time Wade Dempsey had got drunk and in trouble, had seemed to end here. No more alcoholic binging, no more fighting and no more of the philandering that Mary Dempsey had borne with a stoic determination to keep her family together.

They'd had three good years in Azalea Bend. Three years of putting down roots, thinking they'd found home. It was their family's new start. With Wade on the wagon, his genuine passion for the sugarcane fields had landed him the position of plantation manager by that third year. God, Cole had been proud. And maybe, just maybe, he'd hoped even he, once merely the son of a hired hand, would be good enough for the daughter of Maurice Louvel….

But it had been no bright new beginning. Rather, it had been an all-too-lurid end. And when Aimee had died, it had also been all too clear that their acceptance into St. Salome Parish had been the worst kind of mirage.

They were outsiders.

Even Bryn had turned her back on them.

"I'm calling the police," Bryn insisted. "Someone threw a brick through my window. This note is a threat. Maybe they can get fingerprints or analyze it or something."

She sounded so desperate and scared.

"Fine, call the police. But the two of us have already handled the note." Which probably hadn't been the smartest thing to do, but neither of them had been thinking.

"Oh, God." She dropped the note and took a step back. A smear of blood stained the pine floor where she'd stepped.

Reaching out to her without thinking, he picked her up into his arms. The fit of her sexily curvaceous body, the scent of her orange jessamine soap, the feel of her blunt-cut shoulder-length gold hair brushing his cheek, mingled with the magnolia air sweeping in from the broken window, dreamy and nightmarish all at once. How had he teased himself into believing that he could feel nothing for Bryn

Louvel? She evoked a beat inside him as distinctive as a Zydeco rhythm.

And as hard to forget.

"I can walk—" she started.

He knew where the kitchen was located, and even as they left the fulgent glare of the chandelier-lit entry hall, he paced toward it, giving her no time for further protest. Bryn's body felt light, though she'd noticeably filled out since she'd been sweet sixteen.

And filled out in all the right places.

She was tall, slender but toned and far too fascinating with her big, wary eyes and full, kissable lips. She pulled at his heart even as his head told him she was dangerous.

Holding her like this made him remember all too well that there had been tender moments between them. But that had been before their world had spun apart, leaving nothing but bitterness and regret.

Pushing through the swinging door that led into the humongous Bellefleur kitchen, he saw that a light had been left on over the sink. In its ghostly spill, he set Bryn down by the round fruitwood table. She grabbed hold of one of the cane-back carved chairs, putting her weight on the uninjured foot. He pulled back another chair.

"Sit." He headed for the sink.

"Do I need to remind you this is my house?" The chair scraped against the floor as she settled into it. "Who the hell do you think you are? If you hadn't stopped me, I might have gotten a look at that car—"

Cole grabbed a towel by the sink and turned on the water. He looked back at her.

"No, you wouldn't have gotten a look at that car. They didn't have their lights on and they were driving off way too fast. And if they hadn't been and you had seen them, who knows what they would have done next. Someone who throws a brick through your window isn't stopping by for a social call. You could have been hurt, Bryn. You *were* hurt."

And he shouldn't care that she was hurt. She'd trampled his heart fifteen years ago. Yet dark and unnervingly deep, he knew he did care and he fought inside himself to keep it under control. He was here for a reason, and opening his heart to Bryn again wasn't part of it.

He wrung out the wet towel and headed back across the room.

"It's just glass," she said, leaning over to inspect the foot she'd elevated on the next chair. "I'm more worried about the window. And who did it. I've got a phone in the office—"

"Let me take a look. You might need stitches. The brick's not going anywhere. You can call in a minute."

She looked up at him, her face half-hidden in the brooding shadows of the room. Her soft lips were pressed in an unpliable line—whether from pain or stubbornness, he wasn't sure. He flicked the switch on the wall, illuminating the table with the lantern-style chandelier. The room was a rustic, aristocratic melody, from the intricately cast arms of the lighting fixture with its delicate leaf-and-beading details to the collection of colorful plates and jugs crowding the overmantel of the old fireplace. Despite the museum-quality antiques filling the room, it had the lived-in feel of generations of Louvels.

He pulled out another chair and drew it close enough to pick up her foot in his hands, rest it on his lap. The night was warm, but her skin felt cold. He could feel the tension in her body. The pieces of glass in her foot were small, thankfully, but when he pulled the sharp bits out, the blood flow increased. He placed the shards on the scarred, antiqued tabletop and wrapped her foot in the towel.

"Do you have some bandages around here some-where?" He settled her foot back on the other chair.

"There's a first-aid box in the cabinet by the sink," she told him.

He found a white plastic box with a red cross stamped on the top. He pulled out the gauze. She un-wrapped the towel. The bleeding had slowed. She took the gauze and tape from him, clearly preferring to tend to herself.

His gaze followed the line of her slender foot to the delectably curved calf, and higher. She wore light-weight cotton shorts and a slim-fitting boat-neck T-shirt that hugged the supple rounding of her breasts.

He felt again a very sexual and all-too-familiar tug of awareness, and knew he was going to have to accept it. He'd been attracted to Bryn since he was seventeen years old. He couldn't expect that to change just because he was older. His heart might be dead and ruined but his body was in full working order.

But he didn't have to act on that attraction…and couldn't, because too much else *had* changed.

His gaze continued to rise till he found himself meeting her water-hyacinth eyes, as deep a purple as the wild blossoms covering every bayou and swamp in Louisiana. And just as capable of robbing everything they touched of oxygen. For just a second, he thought he saw the same raw hunger that had so unexpectedly seized him.

His chest hurt, and although he wasn't even touching her, he was more aware of her than ever.

She put the gauze on the table. "I'm sorry I snapped at you," she said in a brittle voice. Whatever she was thinking, feeling, it was under control now. If she'd felt that same crackle of awareness, she wasn't going to let it rule her. "I know you were just trying to help. I don't think I'm going to need stitches," she added.

He nodded. "You're going to be fine."

"I was fine before you got here. I'm not fine now." Her eyes accused him as much as her words. "Now you see why you can't stay here, Cole."

"I'm not leaving."

Bryn heard the determination in Cole's voice, and her chest tightened.

They fell into an uncomfortable silence. Around them, the big house creaked and settled.

"What do you really want from me, Cole?"

"I told you I didn't come here to hurt you, Bryn," Cole said. "And it's true." His eyes were deep, fathomless pools. "We need to talk about Aimee. I know it's hard. I know you don't want to even think about it, but we *have* to talk."

He was right. There was no getting around it. Cole Dempsey had come back into her life and turned it upside down in a matter of hours. And he wasn't going to leave without at least saying his piece. And after that— He still might not leave. But sticking her head in the sand wasn't doing her any good.

"All right," she said finally. "But I want to call the police first."

Cole didn't say anything as he followed her out of the kitchen. He took her arm as she struggled to walk on her bandaged foot. The pain was a dull ache compared to the dread licking at her stomach.

They reached the small anteroom off the entry hall she'd turned into a small but comfortable office. She'd colorwashed blue walls and added an eclectic mix of personal mementoes, artifacts and local crafts, yet there was nothing comfortable about it tonight. The silence lay turgid between them as she punched in the number for the police.

"An officer will be here as soon as possible," she

told him as she put the receiver back in its cradle a few minutes later.

He sat across the desk from her in a threadworn velvet wingback chair, and yet he was still far too close. He invaded her space by his mere presence at Bellefleur. An aura of immutable authority exuded from him. No matter what he wore, he would cut a powerful figure with his dark hair, perilous eyes and the solid breadth of his muscular body.

"You want to talk," she said. "So, talk. You have till the police arrive." Since he'd gotten here, he'd been acting as if he was in charge. She wanted to let him know that he wasn't.

She caught the slight narrowing of his eyes, but he let her words pass unchallenged.

"Would you like a drink?" she offered, coolly hospitably. There was a bottle of brandy in the antique cabinet behind the desk. She needed a drink even if he didn't.

The chair swiveled, and she took the bottle down, along with a couple of crystal glasses. She poured them each a glass, returned the bottle to the cabinet and raised the amber liquid to her lips. The brandy burned sweet and warm down her cold throat.

Cole didn't touch the glass she pushed across the desk toward him.

"My mother became seriously ill a year ago," he said in the still thick of the quiet office. "I buried her in Baton Rouge last month."

"I'm sorry to hear that." She truly hurt for him—
but why was he telling her this? It wasn't that she
didn't care, but she was hardly an old friend catching
up on his life story since last they'd met. She'd never
blamed Cole's mother for what Wade Dempsey had
done. If anything, Mary Dempsey was another of
Wade's victims. Still, she wasn't sure what Mary's
death had to do with Cole's return.

How long would it take for the police to arrive?
The conversation had barely begun and already she
wished it was over. She focused on the small bronzed
bust of Alexandre Louvel, one of the first Louisian-
ans to risk his resources turning Creole cane into
sugar and thereby founding the Louvel fortune, standing sentry on a chipped and peeling painted column
by the door. He'd found a way to profit on the lands
he'd inherited, and Bryn often felt his vacant, heavy
gaze as she sat behind this desk and tried to turn
around Bellefleur's future once again.

"I never thought I'd come back to Azalea Bend,"
he said. "I worked my way through college, and on
through law school. I never looked back, not once."

He appeared to be in no hurry to get wherever he
was going with this conversation, and that bothered
her more than anything else. He was confident, composed, while she felt her own control slipping.

Time to cut to the chase and get this done. She
turned her gaze from the bronze of Alexandre Louvel
and squared it on Cole.

"I thought we were going to talk about Aimee." Her hand shook as she lifted the crystal glass and took another sip. "Your father swore revenge, and he took it. Everyone at Bellefleur heard his threats. He went to town and got drunk—a dozen people saw him in the bar, talking crazy. The Louvels were going to pay. And he came back and killed Aimee…because she was the only Louvel he could find." God, and how she blamed herself for that.

She'd been down by the river with Cole that night, both of them desperate and aching. Her sister had offered her comfort, even her help. Aimee had insisted that she could fix everything. But all Bryn had been able to think about was losing Cole. Wade would have to leave Azalea Bend to search for new work, and his family would go with him. She might never see Cole again, despite his promises to write and call. And if her parents found out she was trying to keep in touch with Wade Dempsey's son…

She'd gone to Cole instead. And Aimee had waited for her. Bryn had come back to the house in time to hear her sister's screams. She'd never known for sure where her parents had gone that night, but they'd been fighting and Patsy had driven off in the car. Her father had chased after her. Everything about that night had been awful.

They'd come home around the same time as Bryn. And then things had just gotten more awful.

"Those threats, they were empty words," Cole replied. "He'd been unjustly fired and he went crazy. He got drunk. That doesn't make him a murderer."

"Are you going to tell me why you're here, Cole?" She couldn't take much more. Remembering that night…it always killed her a little more each time. "We had this conversation fifteen years ago, and I can't see one good reason to have it again."

Cole leaned forward, his forearms resting on the solid polished mahogany of the desk that had once belonged to her great-grandfather. His voice lowered, as if meant only for her even when the two of them were alone in the house anyway.

"My mother went to her death wanting to believe my father was innocent—but fearing somewhere inside herself that he was guilty." His eyes bored hard into hers. Emotion lurked in those lithoid depths, but it was unreadable. "She was haunted by that question, Bryn."

She didn't know what to say. Her family had been haunted by that night, too. What was Cole getting at?

She knew he was getting at *something*.

"Before she died, she told me something she'd kept secret all my life. She was pregnant with another man's child when she married Wade Dempsey. He married her and gave me a name, and that's why she stayed with him all those years, even with his philandering. Wade was sterile, couldn't have any children of his own, but he treated me like his flesh and blood and she loved him for that. But she wanted me to know that I wasn't the flesh and blood of a killer. She was ashamed, Bryn, and she didn't want me to be ashamed, too."

"She must have been proud of your accomplishments," she said carefully, shocked by his revelations. Sympathy she didn't dare reveal tore at her heart. "You've made something of yourself. Why should you care what anyone thinks about anything in Azalea Bend now? It's history, Cole. Let it go."

When he continued, it was as if he hadn't heard her. His voice remained oddly flat and expressionless. "I realized I'd let her down, and I'd let down the man who loved me enough to give me his name. The least I could do is try to clear his—not for my sake, but for my mother's. I began to research Aimee's case. Reading documents, police reports. The court transcripts of your father's trial. I read everything I could get my hands on, and one question stood out in my mind."

Bryn's uneasiness increased. His sheer matter of factness continued to prickle alarm up her spine.

She waited.

"My father's face was scratched as if he'd been in a life-or-death struggle that night," Cole went on. "The forensic report was strangely silent on this fact. Scrapings from Aimee's nails should have linked those scratches to my father. But no such evidence was ever presented in court."

"Forensic science was not the same then as it is today," Bryn countered. "This was fifteen years ago, in a small town. We don't have murders in St. Salome Parish on a regular basis. This wasn't a conspiracy, Cole. It was a small town grappling with a big-city crime. If scrapings weren't taken from beneath Aimee's nails—"

"But scrapings *were* taken."

"You just said—"

"I said the evidence wasn't presented in court. I didn't say the evidence didn't exist."

Chapter 4

Bryn swallowed thickly. "What do you mean?" Her voice was a gracile cloak masking unnamable trepidation.

Cole looked at her, his gaze suddenly as frightening as a hot summer storm. "I mean the scrapings were taken. And the evidence was suppressed. The information was removed from the forensic report."

Bryn's stomach muscles clenched. "How can you know this?"

"Because I contacted the coroner who autopsied Aimee's body. I asked him why no scrapings had been taken."

All the blood seemed to run out of Bryn's head.

She felt light, sick. She had to hear what Cole had to say, though. There was no stopping now.

"Randol Ormond is nearly eighty years old," Cole told her. "But he's got all his wits about him. He left Azalea Bend several years ago and now lives in a senior-care center in Tampa. He wasn't hard to track down. I flew there, spoke with him face to face. And he told me the truth. He removed the evidence from Aimee's report—though he wouldn't tell me why or on whose authority. But I can guess."

"Maybe he's lying." Even she knew her words sounded desperate.

"He doesn't have long to live, Bryn. He's got cancer. He has no reason to lie. The truth does nothing but stain his reputation. He's been carrying a load of guilt for fifteen years, and he was only too ready to let it go."

"Maybe he said what you wanted to hear. People change their stories sometimes. People lie for all kinds of reasons."

"I know that only too well." Cole's quiet voice was jeapordous now. "You know as well as I do that your father had more than one reason to shoot mine. And that only one of those reasons would get him out of a jail sentence—and that was pinning Aimee's murder on Wade Dempsey. A jury let Maurice Louvel off for taking a father's justice. But a husband's justice… That would have been a little more difficult to win, even for a Louvel."

Bryn had to force her next words from numb lips. "Did you expect me to tell the world that my mother had an affair with your father? Even *you* didn't believe it was true." But oh, he had wanted her to say it anyway. And she'd refused. And he'd never forgiven her.

A stiff beat passed. "It never mattered what I believed about that, Bryn. It only mattered what your father believed. And you and I both know what he thought that night. We know he didn't fire my father because of negligence on the job. He fired him because he suspected he'd slept with his wife. And when he found my father with Aimee, he shot him dead. After that, there was no backing down. If Wade Dempsey wasn't a murderer, then Maurice Louvel was, wasn't he, Bryn? The town came to Maurice Louvel's rescue. Any evidence that pointed to someone else being Aimee's killer was shoved away because the jury might not have been so sympathetic to the man on trial for murder. Not just the fact that your father had more than one motive to shoot mine. Now there's more. Now there's the forensic report that was suppressed— and who do you think suppressed it, Bryn?"

She felt more ill by the second. She knew where he was headed. Drake's father, the prosecutor responsible for the case against her father. "That's a loaded charge, Cole. And all you have is a grudge and the word of an old, dying man to back you up."

"I have more than Randol Ormond's word." Suddenly the emotion in his eyes was too clear. And it wasn't bitterness or anger. It was pain, pure and scorching. "He still had the original report in his private files, Bryn. He got his daughter to track it down and give it to me."

She could barely breathe. "What does it say?"

"It says that the DNA beneath Aimee's nails didn't match my father's."

Her head reeled, and she grappled for perspective. What if Wade really hadn't murdered Aimee? What if everything she'd believed all these years was wrong?

But everything else she knew about that night warred with Cole's new evidence.

"Mistakes happen," she whispered. There had to be another explanation—

"And so do lies." His face twisted. "It's too late for my mother's peace of mind. I can't do anything for her now. She died while I was in Tampa talking to Randol Ormond. But I can still clear my father's name. Randol Ormond can't be the only one in Azalea Bend who knew the truth about what happened. Someone else fought with Aimee that night, and that someone else fought with my father. I believe my father interrupted the killer, perhaps even tried to save Aimee. I'm here to find out who that was, Bryn. I won't leave till I find out. And I need your help."

Bryn's heart tore. What Cole was suggesting was almost too horrible to contemplate. If there had been evidence to clear Wade Dempsey, evidence that had been suppressed to justify her father's fatal act that night...

Blood roared in her ears. She didn't want to believe any of this. It couldn't be true. "I can't help you."

"Oh yes, Bryn, you can."

She jerked back from the desk. Her chair hit the cabinet and she stood, bracing her weight as much as possible on her uninjured foot.

"My mother has been hurt enough. I'm not going to tell the world that she had an affair with your father to clear a dead man's name. My mother doesn't deserve any more pain. Whatever my father did or didn't think that night doesn't prove anything—"

Cole stopped her as she came around the desk. He rose to his feet, took hold of her by both arms. "That's not what I'm asking of you, Bryn."

"Then what are you asking?" she demanded wildly.

"Nobody asked the right questions fifteen years ago. I'm here to ask them now. And I want answers."

"So what do you need me for?" She shook off his hold. "I can't stop you from asking questions in Azalea Bend. You want to play private detective, go for it. You don't need me. You've even got this supposed forensic report. If there were scrapings taken, have them retested."

Something flinched in his eyes at her obvious doubt. "The scrapings taken from Aimee's fingernails are long gone." He watched her steadily, letting go of her arms but not moving out of her way. "They disappeared when the original report was suppressed.

Someone took them, Bryn. Probably the same someone who suppressed that report. But there was someone else in Azalea Bend who had scratches on their face that night, someone else who had a reason to kill Aimee—and I'm going to find out who it was. But I don't have a prayer without you, Bryn. You're a Louvel. That still means something in this town."

"I can't help you." Her entire being wrenched. She'd spent years trying to put those horrible events behind her. To put Cole behind her. And now that she'd finally started building a new life, Cole was here, asking her to dredge it all up again. "I can't relive the past." And she couldn't believe what he was saying. No one else could have killed Aimee that night. No one else had a reason.

But he wasn't about to let her off the hook. "The original scrapings may be gone, but Aimee's body hasn't gone anywhere. It's in St. Valerie's Cemetery. It's not too late to take new scrapings—"

Oh, God. "No!" Horror washed over her. He was sure she held the key to gaining the answers he wanted, and now she knew just what he'd do to force her to help him.

She could see the small muscle twitching in his jaw.

"I'm sorry, Bryn," he said hoarsely. "I hate this as much as you do." He lifted his hand, brushed his knuckle across her cheek. "I don't want to see Aimee's body exhumed. That's not what I'm asking. There's more than one way to find the truth. But people in this town aren't going to answer my questions readily. They'd answer yours, though—if you help me. We can look for the truth together."

Together. The words seemed to hum in the air between them.

She could so easily fall into those dark-rimmed, soulful eyes, eyes that looked no longer dead but very much alive and hurting, just as she was hurting. In spite of everything he'd just said, his agonized eyes drew her in, made her remember how much she'd loved him....

Bellefleur receded around them, leaving only Cole's eyes, Cole's touch, and the memory of one steamy night by the river's edge...

Her legs wobbled beneath her.

"Bryn..." Her name came out throaty, husky, and he was so close.

Fifteen years vanished. She wanted him, just as she had in those halcyon summer gardens long ago. His lambent magic pulled her in, overwhelmed her, threatened to sweep away her reason. She should hate him right now for shattering her delicate peace, but instead she ached—had ached for him all this time....

A pounding from the front hall jerked through her clouded senses.

Bryn struggled for air, for rationality. She wasn't sixteen. And he wasn't that young boy. He was a man, indurate and cold, and he'd just threatened to have her sister's body ripped from hallowed ground.

She pushed past him, hobbling as fast as possible

to the front door and away from Cole, snatching a pair of sandals from a hall closet on the way.

Officer Martin Bouvier was a couple of years younger than Bryn, but she'd gone to high school with him. He came from a long line of cops, and he did his job methodically, without emotion. He recognized Cole right away.

He took their statements, sealed up the brick and the note in plastic bags, and didn't offer much in the way of encouragement.

"Unless something else happens and we get more to go on, there's probably not much we can do." Martin watched Bryn from the torpid shadows of the portico. He nodded at Cole, standing behind Bryn in the doorway. "How long's he staying?"

Cole stepped forward. He was invading her space again.

"Indefinitely," Cole said.

She gave him a glare, then looked back at Martin. "He registered for two weeks."

"You might want to consider cutting short your stay." Martin's voice was even, non-threatening, but she saw Cole's eyes burn in response, the solar flares lighting within the caliginous green.

"I'm here on business," Cole clipped out. "And I won't be leaving till it's finished."

"Let me know if there's any more trouble," Martin said, directing his words to Bryn before heading down the steps.

The sound of the cruiser's ignition filled the thick night, then faded away as the taillights disappeared up the long drive. Bryn turned back to face Cole.

She could still see the flash of bitter pain in his eyes from Martin's advice. But she couldn't afford to feel sorry for Cole. He'd chosen to come back to Azalea Bend.

He hadn't given her any choice at all.

Bryn stalked past him, leaving him to shut the door. She stepped around the mess of broken glass. She was way too tired to clean it up tonight. All she wanted to do was go back to her bedroom and forget this day had ever happened.

Ha. As if that was going to happen. But she could try. At least till morning, when she'd have to face him all over again.

She used some plastic and tape to seal up the broken window, ignoring Cole. Finished, she headed for the stairs, put her hand on the balustrade.

"Bryn."

She froze for a brief beat. Tension bristled behind her. She could almost feel his eyes on her back, pulling her, making her turn.

His grim visage made her wish she'd kept right on going up the stairs. Damn him for making her feel like the bad guy in this situation. She couldn't stop him from looking for this truth of his, whether he was right about the past or not.

And how could he be right? Why would anyone

else have killed Aimee? Nothing about his claims made sense. Wade Dempsey had been the one with the grudge against the Louvels. The one making threats. The one who'd charged back to Bellefleur drunk, looking for revenge. The one who'd been found with Aimee.

How dare Cole expect her to help him now? She wanted to charge right back down the stairs, shake him, strike him, do something, anything.

Then *he* did something. He closed the space between them in two heartbeats.

"We weren't finished with our conversation," he said quietly. The bright candescence of the chandelier played unforgivingly on his features. God, he was good-looking. Always had been. But now his face was etched with experience, and yet within those austere lines she could still see the boy she'd loved.

His tormented bayou eyes had her aching with a raw need. They'd both given in to that need once and had found something in each other that had seemed too strong to break. But the horror their families had faced had broken it. She'd stood by her family and he'd stood by his. Their youthful trust and love had been shattered irreparably. They'd tried to talk, but they'd both been too hurt and too immature to overcome what stood between them, and eventually it had turned into a bitter chasm. And she wasn't feeling any more capable of overcoming it now. So why did she suddenly wish things could be different?

"Maybe you weren't." She forced her weak knees to move. "But I am."

She left him at the foot of the stairs, but her room was no escape. The pull of him reached her even there. She clicked the lock on the inside of her door-knob and sank onto the night-gloam of her bed.

Sleep was a million miles away, but somehow she found her way into its dark, anguished arms. And the nightmares of Aimee's murder pounded through the wispy night of ghosts and fears.

It was sometime after midnight when a shadow lunged through her bedroom window.

Chapter 5

*B*ryn was screaming.

Cole stumbled out from the rosewood half-tester bed. Sheets tangled around his legs and he almost fell. Bracing himself, he kicked the sheets away and tore from the room. All he could think of was the scream he'd heard the night of Aimee's death. His heart nearly stopped beating and the blood froze in his veins.

The Oleander Room was on the same floor as the room he'd watched Bryn enter a few hours earlier. He raced down the pitch-dark corridor, willing Bryn to be all right, praying in double time. God, if he never asked for anything again, let Bryn be all right.

By touch, he found the door. The knob turned, but the door didn't budge. It was locked.

No sound came from inside Bryn's room now.

Cole pounded on the door. "Bryn! Dammit, Bryn, are you all right? Let me in!"

When she didn't answer, he reared back, prepared to break the damn door down if he had to. The shadow-black of the corridor yawned open as he threw himself against the door.

But his body didn't hit a door. It struck something soft and sweet-smelling. Bryn.

Together, they fell against the hard pine floor. It took a stunned beat for him to realize what had happened, that she'd opened the door just as he slammed forward.

"Bryn, are you okay?" He pulled himself off her. Pale moonlight tracing through her windows sketched her shocked face. Her midnight eyes stared up at him.

"There was someone in my room," she whispered starkly.

The double French doors to the private balcony were shut, the drapes pushed back. Cole reached the doors, flung them wide. The moist air of the Louisiana night enfolded him, soupy and warm. He saw nothing but moon and trees, and heard only the murmur of the river and the rush of leaves in the light breeze. He swung back to Bryn.

She was on the floor, sitting with her knees pulled up, her back braced against the foot of her bed, moon-gleamed blond hair framing her frightened face. Cole knelt beside her.

"I don't see anyone," he told her, crossing the room to crouch down in front of her. "Are you all right? Tell me what you saw."

"I thought I saw someone coming into the room," she whispered again, and he could see tears on her cheeks. He thumbed one away, the satin of her skin cold against his touch. "Oh, God, it must have been a dream."

"We should call the police—"

"No," she cried brokenly. "I've had this dream before. I dream I'm in Aimee's room and someone else is there, too—and I can't save her. I can't stop the shadow from taking her."

In the pale moon, he saw more tears. They fell wet and warm against his hands. He felt like crying, too. He didn't want to feel this connection to Bryn, but it was undeniable.

They shared the pain of that night, whether they wanted to or not. She'd lost her sister. He'd lost his father. And they'd lost each other. Cole closed his eyes against the sudden onslaught of despair inside him.

Opening his eyes again, he sat down beside her, shifting to put his arm around her. He couldn't let go of her.

"I heard you scream," he said.

She drew in a shaky breath. "I'm all right. I'm sorry I woke you. I just haven't had a nightmare like that…in a while."

It was because of him that she was having nightmares now. He'd brought the terrible past back to her. And he'd told himself a hundred times before he got here that he wouldn't care, but damn it all to hell, he cared anyway.

For the first time, he noticed what she was wearing. Or rather what she wasn't wearing. She'd left on the slim T-shirt she'd worn earlier, but had taken off the shorts. A wisp of panty peeked from between her pale thighs in the gloaming night.

He jerked his gaze away, back to her face. She stared back at him with her huge, hurting eyes. She was trembling and without thinking, he rubbed her back, trying to calm her down. He could feel her heart pounding.

"I still miss Aimee," she said then.

Her words broke his dead heart. "I know." He still missed his father. His mother's loss was new and raw. "The pain never completely goes away, does it?"

She shook her head. "We always did everything together. When we were eight, we took swimming lessons. Aimee took a bad dive and hit the board, cut open her forehead. And after that, she wouldn't go back. She wasn't a good swimmer, anyway, and she'd always hated the water."

Bryn and Aimee hadn't been identical, either in looks or personality. They had the same coloring, but Aimee was always smaller, shyer, somehow more fragile. It had been Bryn, with her bright energy, strong body and will and flirty-innocent eyes, who had captivated his attention—and held it.

"She cried and cried because she thought she was letting me down when I wouldn't go on with the lessons without her," Bryn continued. "She knew I loved swimming. But that's the way things were with us. We did everything together, or not at all. Until that last summer."

Cole didn't say anything. He couldn't say anything. He didn't know what to say, how to comfort her. He hadn't known fifteen years ago, either. And she hadn't known how to comfort him. A fresh wash of hurt struck him. They'd failed each other, terribly. It hadn't all been Bryn's fault.

"I loved dreams when I was a little girl," she whispered softly. "I always had good dreams. We loved to feed the brown pelicans down by the river, and I used to have this same dream over and over where I would take Aimee's hand and we'd fly away with them. We'd go anywhere in the world we wanted to go, then we'd come home."

"The two fairy princesses of Bellefleur flying away on wings of pelicans," Cole whispered, still stroking her back, her hair. "I can just see it."

A long beat passed. Her eyes seemed to search his, and he had no idea what she was looking for. She looked achingly beautiful in the gossamer-gleam of her room. She could have been sixteen, she looked so young and vulnerable suddenly.

Then she drew in a deep, shaky breath. "I don't know why I'm telling you this."

"I'm not your enemy, Bryn."

Her gaze held on to him. "Then what are you?"

As he gazed back at her, he saw realization creeping into her eyes. The tension shifted into something else, something nearly electric. And now that the fear was past, the blood thrumming through him was communicating an altogether different need. And she felt it, too. He saw her desire in the glitter of her tear-drenched eyes.

His gaze flicked to her mouth. Her soft lips parted as if in readiness. It had been so long since he'd touched her this way. So long since he'd kissed her.

And yet he remembered exactly how she fitted in his arms. He knew her taste, her slight sigh and the way she tipped her head to the right just as his lips closed on hers.

Her mouth was warm and she made him think of summertime and sugarcane. He remembered her kiss, her innocence, and all these years later she was only that much more intoxicating for not being quite so innocent anymore. He deepened the kiss with all the pent-up passion he'd blocked for so long. Her hands crept up to tentatively touch his chest, and she was kissing him back. He felt the fever in her response, and heard the choked sob in her throat—and he knew she was feeling everything he was feeling. Pain and need and rightness—

And hopelessness and grief.

Suddenly he pulled away from her, and their gazes crashed, dark and wrenching, for what seemed like an eternity. Then she blinked and drew back from him. He could see her retreating, the walls coming back up. Solid and impenetrable.

She wanted him, and he wanted her. And they weren't going to do a damn thing about it. It would hurt too much. There was no going back. They'd gone down this road before and it had ended painfully. They'd been too young, too wounded, too…everything. It was too late to pretend they could start over.

And neither of them had to say it.

"Please just go," she whispered.

And he did.

Insane.

That's what she had to be. She'd freaking lost her mind. She'd let Cole kiss her.

Who was she kidding? She'd kissed him back.

Bryn swept angrily at the scattered glass on the floor of the entry hall, pushing the shards into the dustpan. The pieces glittered in the dawn light streaming through Bellefleur's front windows. She was furious with Cole, but more so with herself. He could invade her house but he couldn't invade *her,* not unless she let him.

And she'd let him.

No more. Lips grimly set, she carried the bin of

shards down the corridor to the kitchen. This morning, the cuts in her foot were but a distant ache. Worse was the sting of regret.

The memory of Cole's burning kiss.

The weakness of that moment in the moon-shrouded bedroom frightened her. How little it had taken to sweep away her resolve. It was as if this one man had the power to switch off her internal controls. And all it took was one fragile beat in the dark for the clock to swing back fifteen years and put her at his mercy.

From now on, she had to keep her head on straight, her heart solidly shielded. The last time they'd been together had ended with disaster, and they could end up right back where they'd started if she wasn't careful. He'd demanded then that she believe his father hadn't killed Aimee, and he was demanding the same thing now. She'd felt as if she had to choose between her parents and Cole, and in her grief, she'd made the only choice she could. He'd threatened, in the most horrifically literal way, to dig up the past. She had a new life for herself and a business to protect and build. His needs had no place in her life.

But what if Cole was right? What if Aimee's killer was still out there?

It was too terrible to contemplate, but she couldn't get it out of her mind. And the real question was what was she going to do about it? He wanted her to help him by revisiting the past, and the mere thought of doing anything of the sort made her feel sick.

And yet somewhere deep inside she feared she'd have no choice—and not because of Cole's threats. How could she live with the knowledge that Aimee's killer could be walking free in Azalea Bend?

She dumped the glass shards in the trash then put away the broom and dustpan. The aroma of baking sweet potato muffins filled the kitchen. Coffee was ready. She should pour a cup, place a muffin and juice on a tray and take it up to Cole's room. It was part of the package at the Bellefleur Bed and Breakfast.

The oven timer dinged. She set the hot sweets on a rack to cool and went to the downstairs office.

It wasn't quite 8:00 a.m. Drake would still be in his apartment overlooking the exotic art deco capitol building. She picked up the phone and dialed his number.

"I'm sorry to call so early," she said when he picked up. "I know you must be getting ready for work."

"Is something wrong?" Drake asked immediately.

"No." Bryn took a difficult breath, let it out. "Yes. It's just that Cole told me something last night. I don't know what to think about it. I guess I want to know what you think." She felt swamped by a sudden reluctance. Cole's mission in Azalea Bend was already tearing her apart. She hated to hurt Drake, too. But Drake had as much at stake in this mystery as she did. The murders and Maurice Louvel's trial entangled all their families. "I want you to tell me it's crazy." She realized as she said the words aloud that it was exactly what she craved to hear. She trusted Drake, and she desperately needed perspective. Drake's father had been dead for several years, but his name was still revered in St. Salome Parish. And Drake's ambitions for the governor's house rested, in part, on his family's reputation.

"What is it, Bryn?"

She swallowed the lump of regret in her throat. "He's here to clear his father's name. He's determined to prove Wade Dempsey didn't kill Aimee. According to Cole," Bryn went on, "the original forensic report from Randol Ormond would have cleared his father, but it was suppressed. And the document was altered."

She didn't have to point out that the person who would have suppressed it was Hugh Cavanaugh.

"My father wouldn't have done that." Drake's voice was curt, but she knew the anger wasn't directed at her. It was meant for Cole. "If he's come back to throw around the same wild charges he made fifteen years ago—"

"Maybe it's not so wild now," Bryn interjected. "He's seen Randol Ormond. Cole says he gave him the original report."

"Have you seen it?"

"Not yet."

"I have a committee meeting this morning, but I'll be at Bellefleur this afternoon."

"Thanks. Wait." The note on her desk calendar

caught her eye. With everything that had been going on, she'd almost forgotten. "I have the St. Salome Garden Club booked for a tea at four. Can you make it before then?" Hiring out the mansion to community groups was one of her latest ideas to generate income.

"I'll be there by one. And Bryn?"

She waited.

"If Cole Dempsey does anything to hurt you, I swear I'll kill him with my bare hands."

Bryn's stomach hurt when she hung up the phone. She'd never heard Drake talk that way before. The brick, Drake, the kiss in the night— She hadn't even told Drake about the brick incident. There was no point in upsetting him more.

Cole Dempsey had been back in town one night and the whole world had already tilted off its axis.

She got up from the desk just as a knock came on her partially open office door. Emile Brouchard looked in, his short, stiff white hair crowning his square-jawed, sun-beaten face. He wore, as usual, a neat pair of workman's overalls with tools poking out of every pocket. He was sixty-five years old, but still vigorous even in semi-retirement.

"Hey, Mr. Brouchard." She attempted to infuse cheeriness into her voice. The last thing she wanted to do was let anyone, even Emile Brouchard, know anything was wrong. He'd managed the Bellefleur grounds for as long as she could remember, until the money had run out and the gardens had fallen into disarray, and even then, he hadn't quit completely. When it had become clear that Patsy Louvel would never come back to the main house, he'd planted her treasured camellias all around the cottage, watering and tending and pruning without ever expecting a dime in pay.

His younger sister Mathilde had been her mother's maid in the old days, and Bryn had scraped together enough cash to hire them both part-time. Emile worked a couple days a week keeping the wilds at bay in the gardens, at least to some degree. Mathilde came in weekly to help with some of the cleaning.

"I knocked on the door, but you must not have heard me," he said. "I saw the broken window. I was worried about you, so I came on in—"

"I left it unlocked for you. We had…an incident last night."

Mr. Brouchard gave her a worried look from beneath his bushy brows. It reminded her of the way he'd looked at her once when he'd found her hiding in the gardens after she'd broken one of the fragile china angels her mother so cherished. Mr. Brouchard couldn't keep her out of trouble, but he could give her a piece of the candy he always had in his pocket and make her feel better for a few minutes.

Candy wasn't going to help now.

"What happened?" he asked.

Bryn sighed. "Just a little vandalism. I think. I

hope." She really didn't want to delve into the details. "I've got muffins in the kitchen," she offered brightly.

"I hear you have a guest," he said narrowly.

"Melodie told me she ran into you last night at the Kwik Pak."

"Cole Dempsey. The boy must be all grown up now." Oh yeah. Cole was all grown up.

"That little incident last night didn't have anything to do with Cole Dempsey coming back to town and staying at Bellefleur, did it?"

There was no point hiding the truth from Mr. Brouchard, she realized with a sigh. He knew too much about her family and Cole's. She could spin the story to visitors who might come to tour the mansion today and see the broken window—it was open weekdays from nine to four, and the tours actually brought in a goodly amount of cash, albeit erratic. But spinning to Mr. Brouchard was a waste of time.

"Someone threw a brick through the window. With a note. Not a nice note, either."

"It's not my place to say it, Miss Louvel, but I'm going to say it anyway. That boy staying at Bellefleur is trouble. St. Salome Parish doesn't forget anything. Or easily forgive."

She thought about the note that had been attached to the brick. It wasn't fair that people blamed Cole for what his father had done, but she couldn't blame him, too. It wasn't his fault. He wasn't responsible for his father's crime.

And she couldn't stop the doubts he'd planted from creeping into her thoughts.

"He's here to clear his father's name," she said softly. "It's not going to get better."

Somehow she wanted Mr. Brouchard to tell her she was wrong. He didn't.

"I can be staying here on the premises for a few nights, if you'd like," Mr. Brouchard offered. "Just in case there's any more trouble."

She shook her head. He was energetic as ever, but he was still sixty-five years old. Somehow, she couldn't quite see Mr. Brouchard being any protection from the town's bitterness toward Cole. "That's sweet," she said, not wanting to hurt his feelings. "But I'll be all right. There aren't many murders in Azalea Bend. I know kids here tell scary stories about the girl who was attacked by a crazy killer one summer night. They say Wade Dempsey's ghost is in the woods and all kinds of stupid stuff. It's our own little not-so-urban legend. No doubt news of Cole's return has reached everyone in town by now. It was probably some bored kid's sick idea of a prank, that's all."

Mr. Brouchard watched her with concern. He wasn't buying that theory. And she wasn't surprised he wasn't happy with Cole staying at Bellefleur. Emile Brouchard had observed firsthand the destruction of her family over the past fifteen years.

Tension tightened her shoulders as she returned to the kitchen. Like it or not, she had to take the tray up to Cole and face him and whatever came next.

Chapter 6

Her feet felt as if they weighed fifty pounds each as she trudged up the steps with the laden tray. She decided just to knock and set the tray on the floor in front of his door, coward that she was. He'd been right that the conversation they'd begun last night wasn't over, but she wasn't in any hurry to finish it. She needed to think. She was still reeling from Cole's charges, the new information about the forensic report. And his kiss.

Particularly, her reaction to it.

Her reaction to *him*.

The door opened just as she lifted her fist to knock.

"Morning." He looked deliciously, adorably rumpled, dressed in faded, worn jeans and nothing else. She had to force her eyes off his bare chest and tamp down the spear of rebellious desire that reminded her that her reaction to him last night hadn't been an anomaly.

"I brought you some coffee, juice and a muffin." He took the tray. Their fingers brushed and his serious eyes caught hers. That was all she needed—more physical contact with Cole. "I'll fix a full breakfast downstairs, if you like. Plantation-style."

"This will be fine. I'm going out early." He watched her, and she could see the concern in his eyes and something else—regret? It was just the faintest flicker, then he turned away to set the tray down. His broad bare back was tanned, as if he spent a lot of time outdoors, which surprised her since he was clearly a successful attorney. But he wasn't spending all his time behind a desk, that was for sure.

He came back to where she stood in the doorway.

"I'll get that window fixed for you," he said.

She blinked, realizing she'd been just standing there, staring at him. Then what he'd said registered.

"You don't have to do that. I'll call someone—"

"It wouldn't have happened if I wasn't here, Bryn."

She couldn't argue with that point, but she didn't like accepting favors from Cole.

"We still need to talk," he added quietly.

"We'll talk when Drake gets here."

His gaze sclerosed. "Drake Cavanaugh?"

She nodded. "He's going to drive in this afternoon from Baton Rouge. He wants to see the forensic report. So do I. We've all got a stake in this, Cole. We'll talk then. Together."

Whether she liked it or not, they did have to talk. For Aimee's sake. But she needed the buffer of Drake's presence. And the perspective of someone she trusted. She couldn't trust Cole. She couldn't trust herself *with* Cole.

"Good," was all Cole said in response.

She had no idea what he was thinking. Then, surprisingly, he told her.

"About last night," he began.

And, oh God, she was pathetic, because her stupid heart wanted to hear what he had to say. What had happened to the pep talk she'd given herself just that morning about keeping emotionally detached? All Cole had to do was open the door and his inky, brooding magnetism reached out and sucked her in. All the rational reasoning in the world couldn't stop her heart from pounding, her palms from sweating.

His gaze seared her, then he said, "It was inappropriate, and I take full responsibility for it. I'm a guest in your home."

Inappropriate? She didn't know how to respond to that. Here she was, her body heating just from looking at him, and he had the composed restraint to refer to kissing her as if it were a mere social faux pas.

She should be glad, dammit, that he recognized

that kiss as a mistake. It would make the next two weeks a hell of a lot easier if he didn't kiss her again.

"I hadn't given it another thought," she managed blithely. "Don't concern yourself."

He wasn't the only one who could play it cool.

Not that her knees weren't shaking all the way down the stairs.

The land rolled out flat and murky on either side of the two-lane highway into Azalea Bend. Crawfish ponds, rice farms and sugarcane ruled here, and the huge Louvel sugar mill still loomed on the horizon just outside town, even though Cole knew the plant had been closed for years, the sugar production moved to another mill fifty miles away.

The Louvels were no longer the biggest employer in St. Salome Parish.

Azalea Bend wasn't suffering from the Louvels' loss, though. Rather, it had been reborn with an annual Zydeco Festival, slated to begin that evening and run through the weekend. More signs along the side of the road promoted historic tours of Courthouse Square. Driving in to the heart of the old town, Cole couldn't help but be impressed by the restoration of numerous commercial establishments and public buildings. The town square had been spruced up with delicate creamy shades of paint and carefully manicured gardens. Many of the buildings displayed signs boasting *Ici On Parle Francais*—French Spoken Here.

But the very fact that Azalea Bend had learned to preserve and feed off its history only reinforced the knowledge that it didn't forget or forgive the past. Cole inched his black Cobra to a stop in front of the J. C. Barrow housewares and hardware store that covered nearly a block downtown. A sense of surrealism overtook him as he walked into the hundred-year-old store. He'd been in the building a thousand times, if he'd been in it once. J. C. Barrow stocked everything from big-mouth cookie jars and cast-iron skillets to galvanized steel and lumber.

He recognized the short-statured old man in the painter's overalls and battered cap near the front even before he turned.

"Good morning, Mr. Wegand." Cole stuck his hand out.

The weathered face of the hardware-store owner creased in confusion as he pivoted and took in Cole's face. His hair had grown whiter over the years, but it still stuck out from his head in the same untamed tufts that, combined with his squinty black eyes, made him look like a cunning elf. He spit a load of tobacco juice in a cup before he set it down on the counter and took Cole's hand in a firm shake.

"Do I know you, young man?"

"Cole Dempsey. Wade's son. Used to come in here with my father all the time fifteen years ago. Before the murder." No sense pussyfooting around. He was there to rock the boat.

George Wegand's eyes narrowed and he ended the handshake abruptly. "Well, you don't say. You're Wade's boy." He studied Cole for a long beat. The sound of men talking in the back of the store filtered toward the front. A clerk at the register watched curiously even as he took an order for electrical supplies over the phone. "Passing through Azalea Bend?"

"Not exactly passing through," Cole replied smoothly. "I'm staying at Bellefleur." That raised a bushy white brow from Mr. Wegand. "I'm a criminal defense attorney in Baton Rouge." He whipped out his business card and held it out. Mr. Wegand didn't take it. "I'm investigating the murder of Aimee Louvel. I intend to clear my father's name. I've got a lot of questions, and I'm looking for people with answers." He laid his card on the counter. Mr. Wegand was getting it whether he wanted it or not.

Mr. Wegand picked up the cup again, kept his dark gaze trained on Cole long and hard, then spat before he spoke. "I'm going to give you a piece of advice because I liked you once and nothing that happened back then was your fault. Folks in this town aren't going to like it if you go around asking questions. Go back to Baton Rouge and forget about Aimee Louvel."

"I'm not worried about what folks in this town like or don't like." Cole knew what people in St. Salome Parish liked. They liked thinking an outsider like Wade Dempsey was the killer. Couldn't have been one of them. "But maybe folks in this town ought to worry about me."

Mr. Wegand shifted the wad of tobacco in his mouth. The clerk at the register put down the phone.

"You got business in my store, boy?" Mr. Wegand asked.

Cole ordered the glass panes cut for the window at Bellefleur then, leaving the Cobra outside J. C. Barrow, he walked into the town. The morning was hot, muggy and as familiar as it was strange. The last time he'd seen Azalea Bend, he'd been driving his father's beat-up Ford truck out of town, his mother beside him, everything they owned piled in the back, the memory of Bryn's eyes haunting him all the way to Baton Rouge along with the thought that he'd never see her again.

Now he'd more than seen her. He'd held her and kissed her. And it was killing him. All he had to do was look at her for shooting darts of heat to stab him straight in the gut. But he couldn't act on that heat, not again. If they got involved, it would be no simple affair. There were too many layers to Bryn and his feelings for her. Bleak, mysterious feelings that were better left dead and buried—for both their sakes.

But in spite of the danger, he needed Bryn.

No matter how much he believed in his father's innocence, he had no idea where to start hunting for the truth. And his conversation with Mr. Wegand was a perfect example of what he knew he'd face all over this town. Stone walls.

The Café Petit Paris was cool, welcoming and deserted at this mid-morning hour except for the old-timers playing bourre in the rear card bar. Cole ordered coffee and watched the men argue over the game. Then he got down to business.

From the Petit Paris, he went to the old fire hall, now a museum, the meat market and even the Zydeco club. He introduced himself everywhere he went—and despite the shocked, often resentful reception he received, he passed out his business card with his cell-phone number, and made certain everyone knew he was staying at Bellefleur.

And he made damn sure they knew why.

Outside the Great House, storm clouds gathered, promising rain. Inside, Cole replaced the broken pane and wiped the line of caulk with a damp towel. He'd worked his way through college doing construction and had discovered an unexpected love affair with restoration while involved in preservation projects in Baton Rouge. It had turned into a continuing leisure pursuit when he'd bought a rundown steamboat gothic home in a shady residential district of the city.

Bellefleur was the antebellum jewel of River Road and not even the ghosts of his youth could take away the pleasure he took in making the minor repair. It was impossible not to appreciate a house that held so much history, even when some of that history had been ruinous. Like the passion and regret he held for Bryn, his attraction to the house was undeniable.

But he didn't belong here. Never had, even though his teenaged self had believed differently. And he didn't belong with Bryn—she'd damn sure made that clear to him. Like Bryn, this house was too much of a hell for him to ever be a heaven.

Cole put down the caulk and towel. He'd swept the bits of glass he'd cleaned out of the window seating into a pile. He hadn't seen Bryn since he'd come back from town, though he supposed she must be about the plantation somewhere.

He wandered into the drape-drawn parlor furnished with matching Victorian rosewood pieces. A kaleidoscope of period clutter filled the room—rococo candlesticks, tall glass odalisques, iron urns. Books burst out of twin-vaulted shelves flanking the hearth. On the walls, family portraits mixed with religious art in antiqued frames, lending a medieval air to the space. Against one entire side hung the family's colorful collection of Mardi Gras invitations. This was Bryn's world of privilege and parties. How had he ever had the sheer arrogance at seventeen to think he could so much as touch one of the princesses of Bellefleur?

Even now, he felt out of place in Bellefleur's rundown, rambling grandeur.

There was a sound from the hall, and he turned back to see Drake Cavanaugh enter the house. He hadn't even knocked. He'd just opened the door and come on in.

A hot twist hit Cole's stomach when, before he emerged from the shadows of the parlor, he heard feet treading down the steps and saw Bryn cross the hall. Cavanaugh put his arms around her. And she let him.

"I'm glad you're here," she said softly.

Cole watched her from the doorway. Cavanaugh met his gaze over Bryn's shoulder.

"Hello, Cole."

Bryn turned. Cavanaugh kept a possessive hand on her waist, Cole noted. With his expensive-cut dark haircut and patrician features, he belonged at a place like Bellefleur with a woman like Bryn. He wasn't an outsider, and he knew it. Drake's sleek gray suit contrasted with Cole's faded jeans and plain T-shirt, throwing them back in time. The son of the prominent St. Salome prosecutor and the hired hand's boy.

And between them, the plantation princess in shorts and a cherry tank top. She had her hair pulled back in a loose ponytail.

"Cavanaugh." Cole forced himself to move forward, hold out his hand. Drake accepted the handshake, moving his touch from Bryn to briefly grasp Cole's hand.

"Let's talk in the library," Bryn said. She looked uncomfortable.

Cole steeled himself against the sympathy tugging

his gut. Sympathy wouldn't get him the answers he needed. If she thought things were uncomfortable already, she had no idea how much more uncomfortable they were going to get.

She'd find out soon enough.

Chapter 7

The library was a rich, solid-feeling space with oak-planked walls and heavy furnishings. Watercolor seascapes and more leather-bound books lined the room. It wasn't hard to imagine the Louvel men of times past drinking brandy, smoking cigars and talking of war and politics while they counted their sugarcane cash.

Not that there was much cash at Bellefleur these days. Cole hadn't missed the empty spaces left on sun-faded walls around the mansion that revealed the stark reality of Bryn's current financial straits. It was clear pieces had been sold to keep the plantation running in recent years.

Bryn settled behind the massive desk. Cole and Drake sat opposite in wingback chairs.

"As you know, of course," she said, "Drake's father was the prosecutor for St. Salome Parish when my father was tried. Drake would like to hear about your visit with Randol Ormond, and we'd both like to see the original forensic report."

Cole was prepared. He leaned forward to reach into his back pocket. Pulling out a crisply folded paper, he opened it and slid it across the desk to Bryn. He gave an abbreviated repeat of the information he'd provided Bryn the night before.

Bryn passed the paper across the desk to Drake.

"This is a copy," Drake said.

"Yes." Cole sat back. "The original remains in my possession." It was safely tucked away in a bank drawer in Baton Rouge awaiting authentication.

"How do we know you haven't tampered with it?" Drake asked narrowly.

"You're free to talk to Randol Ormond for yourself," Cole replied. He refused to rise to Cavanaugh's bait, his implication that Cole was a liar. "He's at the Blue Water Shores Rest Home and Care Center. Tampa."

"It's not much to go on," Drake pointed out, "a copy of the supposed original forensic report, allegedly suppressed fifteen years ago. My father's dead and he can't defend himself."

Cole's gut clenched. "My father never got a chance to defend himself, either."

A viscous tautness filled the room. Bryn broke it.

"This is about Aimee," she said quietly, tensely. Her eyes shone with anguish. Drake reached across the desk and put his hand over hers, and Cole's stomach twisted again. "If there's some chance Aimee's killer is still out there, that's not something I can ignore."

"That's what he wants you to think," Drake argued. "He's playing you, Bryn." He cast a look at Cole. "What if he doctored that forensic report himself? Anything's possible. What better revenge than to come back to Azalea Bend and accuse your father of murder and mine of conspiracy and fraud? That makes a hell of a lot more sense to me than what he's saying."

Cole would have been perfectly happy to knock Drake Cavanaugh on his well-heeled ass. Problem was, he wasn't sure if that urge was instigated by Drake's words or the fact that he couldn't seem to keep his hands off Bryn.

Either way, he was going to have to rely on the icy control he'd spent fifteen years developing or risk losing any hope of gaining Bryn's trust.

"I can guarantee you that I *will* speak to Randol Ormond myself." Drake's menacing look softened as he turned to Bryn. "I've got a couple of fundraisers this weekend, but if I can't get satisfaction on the phone, I'll arrange to fly out to Tampa next week." Now he looked back at Cole. "In the meantime, you want to run around town asking questions, that's fine.

But you start making accusations—that's different. Do we understand each other?"

Cole held Drake's even, glacial gaze. "I'm sure we do." He understood Drake just fine. Cavanaugh was an arrogant rich boy who'd grown up in St. Salome Parish flicking off annoyances like Cole as if they were fleas. And the fact that Cole had shown up at Bellefleur like a bad penny was really pissing Drake off.

And that was fine with Cole. Stirring up the dust was what he'd come to do.

"I've already been in touch with Frank Skelly." Skelly had been the police chief at the time of Aimee's death. Skelly, Ormond and Hugh Cavanaugh had been in the cover-up together, Cole was convinced. So far, Skelly wasn't talking. He'd retired to Atlanta and he'd refused to see Cole when he'd shown up at his door. But he wasn't planning to give up. Ormond had already cracked. Skelly couldn't hold out once the evidence started stacking up. "I'd like to see any personal notes or records your father kept on the case," Cole told Drake.

The air in the room positively crackled.

"I'll look through my father's papers myself," Drake said. "I doubt there's anything of relevance. The court documents are public record."

"Evidence has a way of disappearing," Cole replied. "Just like the scrapings from beneath Aimee's fingernails."

"You're not going to find what you're looking for,

Dempsey." Drake folded the copy of the forensic report and tucked it in his pocket. "This is a fifteen-year-old case. And it's closed. If this forensic report was enough to get it reopened, you'd have gone that route already."

Clean shot. Cavanaugh was right on that score. Cole had contacted the current St. Salome Parish D.A.'s office in the beginning and gotten nowhere. No way was an elected official in Azalea Bend reopening a case involving the Louvels and the Cavanaughs. Especially when the only witness was a dying old man in Florida who was too sick to be brought to the stand. He'd tried the police and had met a brick wall there, too. He was going to need more evidence.

The Louvels might not have the money they once had, but they were respected, and so were the Cavanaughs—and the Cavanaughs still held political sway here. Which was the same reason his threat to have Aimee's body exhumed had been an empty one. But if he could get Bryn on his side…

"I'm looking for the truth," Cole said. "And I'm planning to find it. And if that bothers people in this town, that's fine with me. Someone knows what really happened to Aimee."

Drake didn't just look bothered. He looked furious. "Bryn doesn't want you at Bellefleur."

Cole lifted one eyebrow. "Bryn doesn't want me here? Or *you* don't want me here?"

"I'd like you to know," Drake said tersely, "that I've

asked Bryn to be my wife." His hand was back over Bryn's. "And if you cause her any grief while you're here, I'm going to take it very personally."

Cole's jaw set. He'd known it, sensed it, from the moment Cavanaugh had walked in the door. Drake was too damn comfortable at Bellefleur. He glanced at Bryn. Her heart-shaped face tightened and she pulled her hand away from Drake's touch.

Drake said he'd asked Bryn to be his wife. Had Bryn said yes? Did she kiss Drake with the same sweet fire and passion with which she'd kissed him last night?

"Okay, this isn't going anywhere productive," Bryn said. "Look, I think we can all agree that we need to resolve this issue as soon as possible. I've got a business to build. Drake's got a campaign to run. I'm sure you've got a life in Baton Rouge to get back to."

"Why don't you cut to the chase, Dempsey?" Drake demanded. "I'm not going to just hand over my father's papers. I'll look through them, that's all I can promise. What do you want from Bryn?"

"I want to know who was at Bellefleur the day Aimee died. I want the names of Aimee's friends that summer, the places she went, the things she did. I want to know who might have wanted Aimee dead— and why." It wasn't all he wanted, but it was a start.

Drake's patrician features sharpened in fresh anger. "Aimee was a sixteen-year-old girl. She didn't have enemies."

"Somebody killed her."

"Wade Dempsey," Drake ground back.

Bryn interrupted before the argument could escalate. "I want this settled. One way or the other." She looked at Drake. "He's registered at Bellefleur for two weeks. I'll give him that long." She fixed her heartrending gaze back on Cole. "I'll help you, but in two weeks, if we don't find one single thing to back up your claims, I want you to leave Bellefleur. And I want you to let me and Drake go on with our lives."

Her and Drake's life together? He didn't know if that's what she meant and he didn't like it if it was, but it was a fair enough offer. He'd gotten nothing but cold looks in Azalea Bend this morning. And hell, he'd just been shooting in the dark, anyway. He didn't know where to start asking questions about Aimee. He needed Bryn's help.

As for the two-week time limit, he had no intention of going anywhere until he'd got what he came for. She could toss him out of Bellefleur if she really wanted to, but she couldn't make him leave Azalea Bend.

It was only half a lie to say, "Agreed."

"Are you going to be all right?" Drake's fired-steel eyes held Bryn's with concern. Thunder rumbled overhead as they stood on the steps of Bellefleur. The air was thick with the coming rain.

Bryn nodded. "I'm fine. Thanks for coming."

"You're not alone, you know." Drake touched her

cheek, grazed it lightly with the tips of his warm fingers. "I've got a dinner in the city tonight, but if you need me, all you have to do is call."

A lump grew in Bryn's throat. She appreciated Drake's support, but she knew she had to tread carefully. She didn't want to hurt him.

"You're a good friend," she said softly.

"You know I want to be more than a friend," he answered. He dropped a gentle kiss on her mouth.

She wanted—God, how she wanted—to feel something, the same incontestable sizzle she felt when Cole kissed her. Even a fraction of it. Drake was perfect. Safe. Kind. Dependable. She'd known he would come here today and make her feel in control again.

Cole made her feel out of control.

But Drake's kiss made her feel nothing but a gossamer tangle of regret. She pulled away.

"Drake—"

"I know. I said I'd give you time."

"You shouldn't have told Cole you'd asked me to marry you," she said carefully. "You made it sound as if we're engaged."

"I want us to be engaged," he said, his voice quiet, his gaze so serious.

"I promised you I would think about it, and I have," she told him, her throat thick. She drew in a steadying breath, let it out. She didn't want to lead him on, and she realized she had already, just by agreeing to consider his proposal. Somehow, now, it seemed so clear. "You know how much I value your friendship— but that's not enough to make a marriage. It wouldn't be fair to either of us, but especially to you." It was so hard to say the words, but she had to say them, for his sake. And she had to say them now.

The look in his eyes was hurt, and she hated that.

He was silent for a long beat. "I value your friend-ship, too," he said finally. "I don't want to lose that. No," he said when she started to speak. "It's all right. I know this is a difficult time for you. I didn't mean to make it more difficult." He reached for her hand, squeezed it gently. "We're good friends and that's not going to change."

She hoped that was true, but she felt so awkward now.

"Hey," he touched his hand beneath her chin gen-tly. "Everything's going to be all right. We're fine. And everything else is going to be fine, too. Cole *is* crazy, you know. At the end of two weeks, you'll see that. We're going to be okay."

He was telling her what she'd wanted him to tell her. So why didn't she believe him? She had more rea-son to trust Drake than she had to trust Cole, but every time she thought about Aimee's killer still walking around in Azalea Bend…

"I hope so," she said.

She watched Drake get in his car and drive away. Wind rustled through the antebellum oaks, and Bryn turned back toward the house.

Cole met her with brooding eyes. All strong, dark, tense and masculine. He took over the porch, just as he'd taken over the library by his simple act of being there.

She moved across the portico toward him. Nothing could kill this intolerable wanting she felt whenever she looked at him, but she could—*would*—control it.

"Thank you for fixing the glass," she said.

"If you tell me where you've got a broom and a dustpan, I'll clean up after myself."

"I'll take care of it." Just go away, she willed him. But of course he didn't do any such thing.

He followed her inside where the mess of glass he'd scraped out of the window casings was piled on the floor, and when she returned with the broom and dustpan, there he was, waiting. She swept the glass into the dustpan, and dumped the glass bits into a trash bag.

"So you're engaged to Drake Cavanaugh."

She swung around, dustpan still in hand. His statement lingered heavily in the air like the rumbling echo of thunder from outside.

"We've discussed it. But, no, we're not and we're not going to be, if you have to know. He's a friend, a good friend, but that's all. What's it to you?" God, that sounded childish. What did she want him to say? That it was everything to him, that he cared who she was involved with, that it should have been him she was planning to wed?

"I told you I'm not your enemy, Bryn." He moved closer, his raw sexuality further invading her space.

Her chest tightened and a suffocated feeling intensified.

"You're not my friend either." She made the statement flat. Cole could never be her friend. Her sweetest nightmare, maybe. Her most unattainable taboo. But not her friend.

Two weeks suddenly seemed like a very long time. How she would stand it, she didn't know. Just looking at Cole aroused old tender, hungry feelings that had no place in the here and now.

"I'm sorry that you feel that way, Bryn," he said slowly, watching her.

Did he really think they could be friends? Or was he playing her, as Drake said?

It had probably been insane to promise to help him in any way. All he had was a piece of paper that might or might not be genuine, and on that basis alone she'd agreed to let him drag her back into the worst period of her life. He was using her guilt and grief for Aimee to get his way. And for that reason alone, she couldn't trust him.

"It doesn't matter how I feel," she said tensely.

He gave her a long look. "All right. Then let's get to work."

"I hope you aren't expecting me to jump to your command for the next two weeks," Bryn said, still standing there stiffly. "Because that's not going to happen."

Cole had no doubt that Bryn's agreement to work with him was made reluctantly.

"You want to know the truth about Aimee's death," he reminded her. "And so do I." He watched her as she rested the dustpan on the floor in the corner. She looked every bit as brittle as the glass she'd swept away. "You set the time limit, not me. I'm not planning to waste a single hour in the next two weeks."

"Let's get one thing straight." Bryn placed the broom beside the pan and eyed him squarely. "I'm not convinced we don't already know the truth about Aimee's death."

She wasn't giving in easily to his theories or his new evidence, and he didn't expect anything else. To accept that her sister's murderer had been walking free in Azalea Bend all these years had to be the worst kind of anguish. She was clinging to her shreds of denial for all she was worth.

But he was equally determined to keep things moving forward.

"I need that list I mentioned. People who were at Bellefleur the day Aimee died. Her friends. What she did, where she went that summer," he said. "We'll take it from there."

He was leveled with a hard look. "I'm running a business here, in case you've forgotten. I do have other things to do today."

"And I appear to be your only guest at the moment, so I don't think you're that busy. Unless you're trying to back out of our deal before we even get started."

He watched the ice flash in her eyes. She was good and stressed-out by this whole situation, and ready to take it out on him. Now he knew what water hyacinths looked like at zero degrees.

Did those beautiful eyes of hers ever melt for Drake Cavanaugh? They might not be engaged now— or ever would be, according to Bryn—but he'd bet that wasn't the way Cavanaugh wanted it. Jealousy was not an emotion with which he felt comfortable. In truth, he'd never thought of himself as a jealous man. But Bryn brought out emotions he didn't expect.

"I'm sure the fact that I'm struggling is satisfying for you. How low the Louvels have sunk—literally bringing in boarders to pay the light bill. And I'm still barely making it from one day to the next."

She didn't look angry suddenly. She looked sad, and a little bit scared. Not that she would want him to know that. He could see the struggle within her to contain her feelings, hide them, control them.

"There's no shame in honest work," he said.

"I'm not ashamed."

But, oh, she was. He could see it in the way she didn't quite meet his gaze now. She was a Louvel, born and bred to a brand of luxury and aristocracy that most people—-especially Cole—couldn't begin to imagine. An antebellum birthright that was as out of step with modern times as hoop skirts.

And she was dealing with it. He couldn't help but be proud of her, knowing the way she'd been raised and seeing how she was managing the hand dealt her now.

He wasn't the only one who'd discovered strength in the murky disaster of their shared past.

"Hey." He should have resisted, knew it was a mistake, but his resistance was so unsteady when it came to Bryn. And there was something brimming inside him that he had to say, whether it was wise or not.

He closed the breath between them and touched the silken line of her jaw, capturing the silvery violet of her complicated gaze. He experienced the inexplicably persistent pop of awareness that such nearness to her yielded. "Not much surprises me anymore, but you do. You're a lot tougher than I ever knew."

Her shrug rippled the light cotton of her cherry T-shirt. "You never really knew me, Cole."

The words were stark and unbearably true. What had he known about the girl he'd fallen for so hard and fast? They'd been all fumbling kisses and breathless handholds back then. And one star-lanced night he'd never forget. Adolescent dreams and magic, more fantasy than reality.

She was an adult now, and so was he. And he saw her in the harsh light lent by maturity. She was no fairy princess anymore. She was a woman stamped by some of life's most bitter trials.

And this was just the beginning of yet another trial. For both of them.

"My loss," he murmured, and he meant it.

Her eyes reflected a confusion he understood—he was confused, too. Every time he looked at Bryn, the bitterness that had been his lifeboat all these years sank a little deeper.

She broke the staticky moment by stepping away from his touch.

"Let's just get this done." She turned away, moved toward the anteroom she used as an office. "Believe it or not, I do have work to do today. The St. Salome Garden Club is holding a tea here this afternoon. And as you are aware, I need the income."

His fingers felt chilled as he dropped his hand to his side and followed her stiff, proud back into the office. She sat behind the desk and slid open a drawer to pull out a legal-sized pad. She took a pen from a silver cup on the desk and began jotting down names.

He sat down across from her and waited.

"The regular household staff consisted of Nellie Brewer, the cook, and Mathilde Brouchard, the maid. My mother brought in extra help for dinner parties or special occasions, but nothing out of the ordinary was going on the week Aimee died. Emile Brouchard managed the grounds."

She looked up from the list she was creating. "He hired boys from town every summer to work the gardens. My father kept meticulous records of the plantation accounts, but you'll have to give me time to dig those up. There should be a record of the checks written to yard boys that summer. And of course, there were all the people who worked in the sugarcane fields. They came up to the house sometimes."

Bryn seemed perfectly focused, speaking as she continued to write. "Emile and Mathilde Brouchard still work for me, and as far as I know, Nellie Brewer still lives in town. The sugarcane records are in storage, so I'll have to get that information for you later. Some of those workers were migrants, of course. Look," she glanced up at him again, her pen stilled, "I don't know what you expect people to remember after fifteen years."

"What do you remember, Bryn?"

The look that entered her eyes tore out his heart. He saw the way she fought for control, the way she squeezed her lids for just a beat as if holding in tears.

"It was a normal day," she said quietly. "Just like any other day that summer. Aimee and I slept late. We had pancakes in the kitchen that Mrs. Brewer had kept wrapped in the oven for us. She always kept breakfast in the warmer for us in the summers. We went into town for dance lessons. We'd just gotten our licenses. Aimee drove. We went to the drugstore afterward and shopped for makeup. I bought a new lipstick, then we came home."

"Was there anything different about your parents that day? Any strange people who came to the house?"

"No. Of course, we weren't there all day, but everything seemed normal to me, nobody was there who wasn't always there. When we came back, Mrs. Brewer had set out the afternoon tea and the mail. She would leave the tray on the table in the front hall and Mathilde would carry it up. It was a totally ordinary day."

"What about Aimee? What was she doing that summer? Who was she seeing?"

"We had the same friends, and a lot of their parents were friends of our parents. Like Drake. Our best friends were Dana Kellman and Lizzie Cornelius. Dana's married and lives in New Orleans. Her name is Dana Bleeker now. Lizzie teaches here in town. They were taking dance that summer with us."

"Do you remember who else was in your dance class?"

Bryn frowned in thought then jotted down several names. "I'm not sure who else. It was a small class. I don't know what they're all doing. I know Erica Saville runs a little boutique downtown—the Fleur de Lis."

"How did Aimee spend the afternoon?"

He knew how Bryn had spent the rest of that day. She'd come down to the sugarcane fields and they'd slipped away together to hold hands and share kisses by the river. The memory rushed him, poignant and bitter.

"I don't know what Aimee did that afternoon. I know she took the tea tray up to our mother's room after we got back from dance. Aimee liked to have tea with her sometimes—I hated it—and Mathilde wasn't around, so she took it up. She promised me she was going to tell our parents that I'd twisted my ankle at dance and wouldn't be coming down to dinner so they wouldn't notice I was gone. Then—" She took a ragged breath, and he could see her battling to control her emotions. Was she thinking of that last afternoon by the river, too? She continued, glossing over that part of her day. "Then you walked me back to the house and we heard my parents fighting."

She didn't have to tell him what had happened then. Maurice Louvel had been convinced his wife was having an affair with Wade Dempsey. Cole's father had been called up to the plantation and fired. And being fired meant that he was being thrown out of the little house on Bellefleur land that they'd made into a home. They would have to leave Azalea Bend.

Bryn had been in tears. Aimee had come outside and found them, and she'd been crying, too.

"Aimee said she was going to fix everything," he reminded her quietly. He knew this was the last time she'd spoken to Aimee and it had to be painful, but he had to ask. "What did she mean?"

"You know how she was with us. She thought she was like our fairy godmother, always helping us sneak away. She was going to talk to our mother. I'm sure she thought there was some way she could fix it so your family didn't have to leave Azalea Bend. So you and I wouldn't be separated." She took another shaky breath. "But my mother had driven off, and my father drove after her. Then we went down to the river again."

And when they came back, Aimee was dead.

She'd been outside, probably waiting for Bryn. Cole and Bryn had heard her scream across the plantation, as had her parents from the front of the house where they'd just driven up. But by the time they'd reached the reflecting pool, it had been too late.

The attack had been swift and brutal. Aimee had lived long enough to scream, long enough to fight, but she hadn't had a chance. She'd been shoved down against the edge of the pool, her head striking the decorative rocks that surrounded it. Blood had been everywhere.

Wade Dempsey had been found holding her lifeless body. Maurice Louvel had torn inside and come back with a gun.

All hell had broken loose.

A long, achy silence weighted the room.

"What else was Aimee doing that summer? Who else did she hang out with?" Cole probed gently.

Bryn let out a frustrated sigh. "We went to dance. We hung out with our friends, went to the movies. There were a few other girls from school, that's it. We spent most of our time at Bellefleur. Aimee was a real homebody."

Aimee had been shy, quiet. It had been bright, outgoing Bryn with her engaging smiles and innocent charm who had caught Cole's attention. He'd never gotten to know Aimee, but oh how he'd wanted to know Bryn. There'd been something irresistible about her then. And now.

She scratched down several more names. "That's all I can think of. And I don't know what you think you're going to find. There was nothing deep, dark and secretive about Aimee. She certainly never did anything that would make someone want to kill her."

"But someone did kill her."

"I knew Aimee," she said in a low, heart-rending voice. "We were twins, Cole. We weren't just close in the way normal siblings are close. We knew everything about each other."

"You were distracted that summer."

A slash of guilt darkened her shining eyes. Bryn had spent a lot of time with him that summer. A lot of time away from Aimee. Had she known her sister as well as she thought?

"I knew my sister," she bit out.

"I'd like to talk to your mother, too."

Something unreadable passed through the eyes she shifted away from him. She pushed the list across the desk to him, then raised her controlled, pain-hardened eyes. "I do have work to do here, Cole. Even if it doesn't look as if I do. And I'll talk to my mother alone. I don't want you upsetting her."

He knew when he'd pushed enough. For now. He

took the list she'd made. "Thank you for your help, Bryn." He watched her for a long beat and stood. "My father didn't kill Aimee. And I'm going to prove it."

Rain pounded down outside, obscuring the tall window behind her with a funereal pall. The long-threatening storm had arrived.

Chapter 8

The umbrella popped open beneath the sheltering portico, the sound drowned by the lashing drops of the cold deluge all around. It was a hell of a day for a garden club tea, and she could only pray they didn't cancel. Bryn rushed down the front steps of the house, then slowed in spite of the driving downpour. The brick-lined path to her mother's cottage loomed before her.

Behind her, she'd left Cole, but the tumbling mix of feelings and questions came with her. *You're a lot tougher than I ever knew.* Well, she had him fooled. She was weak. A puff of smoke in the wind, swayed into an emotional morass by his every glance. *I'm not your enemy.* A traitorous part of her wanted to believe that was true. But everything about his presence at Bellefleur confused her. She couldn't trust him, but he had her backed into a corner about Aimee. The one thing she couldn't ignore was the haunting doubt he'd planted about her sister's death.

The cottage was a warm beacon in the darkling afternoon, set amongst the tumbling ruins of other outbuildings—the long-ago separate kitchen, the cotton press from the earliest days of Bellefleur, and the long barracks that had once housed slaves. Her mother's home was one of two restored buildings still in use on the grounds. Double-bloom pink camellias drooped beneath the weight of the pouring rain, surrounding Patsy's cottage like a sweet, sad embrace. Mr. Brouchard planted more every year, and cutting their blooms was the one thing that would bring Patsy Louvel into the sunshine and fresh air. All through the spring of every year, she kept a fresh camellia in a small vase in the midst of her bone china angels.

Formerly the residence of the plantation cook, the two-bedroom turn-of-the century gingerbread-trimmed house was just the right size for Patsy and her companion, Emmie Layton, who was everything from friend to maid to nurse rolled into one. Through the window, Bryn could see her mother sitting by the small hearth, a magazine tumbled back on her lap as she watched the flickering television screen in the corner.

Bryn closed her umbrella in the shelter of the porch overhang and knocked, then pushed the door open a crack. "Mom?"

Patsy Louvel turned in her seat. Her look was gently vague, and Bryn's heart fisted.

"It's me, Mom. Bryn."

"Hello, Bryn. Would you like to come in?"

It was always a question as to whether or not Patsy knew her. Bryn wasn't sure now. Sometimes she was Bryn, her daughter. Other times she was a neighbor dropping by for afternoon tea. Sometimes she was a complete stranger and her mother would become angry and order her away.

Today, Patsy lowered the volume on her soap opera then got up to give Bryn a hug. Maybe today she knew Bryn was her daughter. "I'm just having some tea and watching my stories. Sit down, darling, and I'll get you a cup."

Bryn gave her mother a kiss on her still-smooth cheek, then propped her umbrella by the door. With Patsy's movie-star platinum hair, ruby lipstick and stick-thin figure, she was in most outward ways the woman she'd always been. Her mother rose every morning, dressed as if she were still running a great house, then sat down for hours of game shows and daytime dramas.

That was a good day for Patsy Louvel. On bad days, she didn't get out of bed. Depression had been Patsy's constant foe for years, and the only good thing about the vascular dementia that had made its slow claim on Patsy's mind following a series of small strokes was that most of the time now Patsy Louvel didn't remember Aimee at all.

Her mother made her awkward way to the kitchen for the kettle, spilling as much tea as made it into the cup as she poured, then returned to hand the cup to Bryn.

"Thanks, Mom." Bryn held the china cup in her chilled fingers.

"That'll warm you right up." Patsy sat back down.

The tea was cold, but Bryn didn't point that out. It was just one of a hundred little things that her mother no longer noticed.

Emmie bustled in from the back wearing one of her standard brightly colored outfits. Her dark face dimpled with the ever-present cheerful smile that hid what Bryn knew to be a stubborn efficiency that made a world of difference when it came to tending the often-difficult Patsy Louvel. Patsy had occasional fits where she'd fire Emmie and tell her to pack her bags. Bryn would smooth things over and remind her mother how lucky they were to have Emmie. Bryn couldn't manage without the live-in nurse, even if she could ill afford the expense.

"I thought I heard someone come in." Emmie's shrewd black eyes honed in on Bryn's cup and she frowned. "Let me boil some fresh water in the pot," she said, heading for Bryn's cold tea.

"I'm okay. It's fine." She forced a smile. "I just need to talk to my mother for a few minutes."

"Well, then, I was catching up on some ironing," Emmie said. "Let me know if you need me." She gave another smile and bustled back out, leaving the faint scent of starch behind her.

Rain came down in a relentless pattering. The room lay in an ethereal calm with its shifting shades of blue, from the needle-pointed pillows to the delicate toile walls. An ornately framed mirror reflected the gray of the day outside. Bryn took a deep breath, let it out.

"We have a guest at Bellefleur, Mom." How much her mother was going to grasp of what she was about to tell her, she didn't know. But she had to know if her mother remembered anything that might provide a clue to the truth of Aimee's murder.

"I hope Clint and Rianna are going to work it out this time," Patsy said. "It's just not fair the way they torture them. First he was kidnapped, then Rianna thought he was dead. And now he's back and they still won't let them get together."

It took a few seconds to compute that her mother was talking about the characters on the soap.

"Mom—"

"Did you see what happened?" Patsy interrupted. "She thought he was killed in that nightclub fire, but he wasn't. He's been in a private hospital all this time. He had plastic surgery, and now he's back. Only Rianna's married to Brandon."

Apparently, today, Patsy was living in soap-opera land.

"Mom. We need to talk."

Patsy turned her blank eyes on Bryn. "Of course, darling. I thought we *were* talking."

Her mother looked so damn beautiful and healthy on the outside. But Bryn knew that was only a surface mirage, and what she had to explain now was going to be upsetting if her mother actually understood it. The ball of stress in her stomach constricted.

There was no way to say it right, no way to make Cole's presence more palatable.

Bryn reached out to rest a hand over her mother's. "The guest at Bellefleur is Cole Dempsey."

"Cole Dempsey? Who is that?"

"He's Wade Dempsey's son," Bryn explained patiently. "He's an attorney now, in Baton Rouge. He's been investigating Aimee's death, Mom."

Patsy sank back in her chair, her pale pink manicured fingers sliding out of Bryn's hand. Did she understand what Bryn was saying?

"You know he never believed his father was guilty," Bryn continued. "And now he says he has new evidence—the original forensic report that was never produced at trial. It shows there were scrapings taken from beneath Aimee's nails, and that the DNA didn't match his father's."

The flare of sharp pain in Patsy's vague eyes gave

Bryn hope. "What does that mean?" Patsy asked in a thin voice.

"What he's saying is that Aimee struggled with someone else that night. Not Wade Dempsey. And that maybe Wade Dempsey even interrupted the killer, and tried to save Aimee." She leaned further toward her mother, recapturing her hand. Patsy's fingers lay limp and frail in hers. Trembling. "If Aimee's killer is still out there, we have to find him. Mom, do you have any idea who else might have killed Aimee?"

"Wade Dempsey killed Aimee." Her mother spoke automatically, and Bryn's heart tore at the pain in her broken voice. But she had to take advantage of this moment of lucidity. She had to know if there was anything her mother hadn't told her.

"What if he didn't? What if Aimee's murderer has been free all this time? Did you ever think anyone else could have killed Aimee?"

Patsy was staring at the television again, and there were tears tracing down her cheeks. She didn't say anything.

"Mom," Bryn whispered, "do you remember anything you and Aimee talked about that last day, when she brought the tea up to your room?"

Bryn felt tears brimming her eyes. Maybe if she'd spent that last afternoon with Aimee, she'd have known what happened.

"She was upset about the baby," Patsy said.

Bryn blinked. "What?"

Patsy looked at Bryn. The unsettling vagueness was back in her eyes. "If Rianna hadn't found out she was pregnant with Brandon's baby, she'd have told Clint she still loved him."

Oh, God, she was talking about the show again.

"Have you done your homework, darling? Tell Aimee to brush her teeth."

A shiver swept down Bryn's spine. The worst was when her mother slipped back into the past.

"I'll go do my homework now," Bryn said softly. A long painful beat passed. "I'm sorry, Mom."

Before she left, she took a few minutes to go back to her mother's room where Emmie was stashing folded laundry in her mother's armoire. She explained about Cole and asked Emmie to call if her mother showed any signs of being distraught about it later when she thought about it again. If she remembered it.

"It's getting worse, isn't it?" Bryn knew she didn't need to specify what she meant.

Emmie's dark eyes saddened. "Yes. I'm so sorry, honey."

The big house waited for her with oppressive gloom despite the activity that had begun in her absence. A bakery truck was pulled around back through the carriage entrance. Melodie's cute little Volkswagen bug was parked on the side, next to Bryn's old Chevy Nova. The garden club was responsible for supplying their own food. Bryn was supplying the tea, china and service, and location.

Originally, the party had been planned for outdoors, but with the weather, it would need to be shifted to the front parlor. She was just relieved to find no blinking message on her phone telling her the tea had been cancelled. This was her first community hosting event and she needed it to go off without a hitch.

The last thing she needed was Cole Dempsey in the house.

Cole slipped off a pair of reading glasses as he snapped shut the St. Salome Parish phone directory. He'd found addresses and phone numbers for a good percentage of the names Bryn had supplied. He'd have to track down some of the girls they'd hung out with that summer, find out their married names and where they lived if they'd moved away. Bryn had given him what information she had, but she'd lost track of some of her and Aimee's friends, and he'd have to wait till she had time to dig out the other records she'd promised that were in storage.

For now he'd start with the ones he'd found in the directory. The next step was contact, but he didn't intend to make it by phone.

Voices drifted in through the barely cracked bedroom window between claps of thunder, followed by the sound of a door crashing shut and a truck lumbering away. He'd seen some kind of delivery vehicle come around to the back while he'd been going through the directory.

He realized he was starving. He hadn't eaten anything since Bryn's sweet potato muffin and coffee this morning. Coming downstairs, he noticed the parlor was dark and quiet, but as he headed into the kitchen, he found a hive of activity. Several blue-haired old ladies chattered away as they placed petit fours, crustless sandwich wedges and pastel-colored mints in silver trays and bowls. The aroma of rich tea filled the air.

Bryn looked over her shoulder as she poured the steaming brew into an elaborately-footed silver pot. Rose-patterned china cups were stacked on the old fruitwood table. Someone had filled several earthenware jugs and glass vases with a profusion of flowers in fuchsia and yellow.

The chatter stopped and the faded curious eyes of the ladies in their floral dresses and colorful hats nailed him.

"I was looking for a sandwich," he said.

"Are you ready for me to set up the parlor?" Melodie asked, breezing in from outside. The rain had slowed to a light tapping, and her short hair was wet and frizzed.

"Yes, thanks," Bryn told her. "Start with the trays and I'll be right back to help you with the china. Excuse me, ladies. I have a guest." She put down the pot and dragged Cole by the arm.

She didn't look excited to see him. Not that this was a surprise.

"Your guest is welcome to help himself to our refreshments," one of the ladies said, nodding at the tray of sandwich wedges.

"I was hoping for a man sandwich," Cole said in Bryn's ear, inhaling her delectably sweet jessamine scent as she continued pulling on his arm.

"We don't have any man sandwiches today," Bryn hissed, dragging him completely out of the kitchen now. "We're having a tea. A garden club tea. And the bed and breakfast accommodations don't include any meals other than breakfast. You'll have to go out."

"I guess this means you don't want to introduce me to the garden club," he said teasingly, enjoying himself. Bryn's hair was mussed, stray wisps coming out from where she'd tucked it behind her ear, and she had a smudge of something white on her nose that looked very lickable.

"Not really."

They'd stopped in the corridor between the kitchen and the foyer because he'd dug his heels in before she could drag him another step. He reached up and wiped away the creamy smudge off the tip of her nose. And wanted to do more than touch her. He couldn't look at her without remembering their kiss—and the rebellious heat between the two of them that hadn't died when Aimee had.

"I was helping take out the petit fours," she said,

brushing her own hand over her nose to check for any remainders. "I must have gotten some of the icing on my fingers and then— Anyway, please go," she said in a lowered voice. "This is important to me. To the future of Bellefleur."

He noticed the slight puffiness around her eyes. Had she been crying?

"Did you talk to your mother?"

Her expression tightened. "I can't discuss my mother right now. I really have a lot to do."

"Let me help."

She shook her head almost violently and stepped away from him. "No."

"I just meant, let me help you set up. I can take some of the load off Melodie in getting all those trays carried in to the parlor." He noted her continued hesitation. "You could use some extra hands, and I'd be happy to help."

He meant his offer sincerely. She was under a lot of pressure and it was getting to her more than she liked if the strained redness in her secret eyes was any indication. And her stress was getting to him more than he liked as well.

"Look, we're talking the St. Salome Garden Club here," she went on tensely. "Trust me, they don't *really* get their hands dirty in their gardens. But they do spend a lot of money and hold a lot of prestigious events. It's a coup for me to get them to hold one of their teas here. These are ladies from some of the best families in Azalea Bend. The rest of them will start arriving any minute. I don't want your help. Don't you get it? I don't want you here at all."

A conflicted shadow crossed through her complicated eyes, reminding him that she was hurting, that she was confused and torn apart by what he'd come to Azalea Bend to do. But an old fire coiled in Cole's chest nonetheless. Her words wrought a stabbing reminder of what his place had always been in this town, whether she'd meant it that way or not.

He didn't quite succeed in keeping the bitterness from his voice. "I think I get it, Bryn."

With that he turned and left.

Chapter 9

She felt like a heel and she hated herself for the weakness. Cole had offered to help, and she'd treated him like a leper—which was what he deserved for the way he'd stormed into her life. Yet she didn't like the way her behavior made her feel.

Add to that the pressure of Cole's claims about Aimee's death, the hovering ordeal of her mother's condition and the ever-present concern about Bellefleur's future…

No wonder she was ready to crack. Just one Moon Pie was definitely not going to be enough tonight. The tea had gone well after Cole had left, but she was just exhausted.

In fact, she was on her third chocolate-covered, marshmallow-filled cookie sandwich when she heard him come in. The rain had stopped hours ago, leaving the house eerily quiet. Half of her prayed he'd go straight upstairs to bed, and the other half— Whoa. What the other half of her wanted was scaring the daylights out of her.

He walked into the kitchen and she could see him taking in the scene. Empty cookie pie wrappers and Bryn sitting all alone in the shadowy room, the only illumination coming from the light over the sink. He didn't say anything for a long beat, then he grabbed a cane-back chair, flipped it around and straddled it.

"Moon me, baby."

She had to laugh, almost choking on the bite of gooey chocolate and marshmallow in her mouth in the process. She managed to swallow it down.

"Help yourself."

"Sure you want to share?" he asked. "I don't want you to go hungry or anything."

There was a twinkle in those hard eyes of his, or maybe it was just the bulb flickering in the light over the sink, about to burn out.

"Shut up. I'm pigging out. Stop me." She shoved the whole box of Moon Pies at him.

He took one out and unwrapped it. "Want me to put the rest of these away to save you from yourself?"

She laughed again, and it felt good. She hadn't laughed much lately. "Please."

Cole put the box of goodies on the kitchen counter near the sink then came back, straddling the chair again. "There you go. You're safe now. So how'd your tea party go?"

"Fine." She watched him take a bite of his Moon Pie. Then she watched him lick a crumb of cookie from the corner of his lip. Safe? No, she was far from safe. Not with Cole here, all sexy and delicious-looking and not angry as she'd expected him to be. Why didn't he ever look like a stiff, proper lawyer? In his jeans and black T-shirt, he looked like a bad boy instead, all steamy sexual energy and dangerous, pinning gazes. She tried really hard to focus. "Did you get something to eat?" She wanted to ask him what he'd been doing for six hours. It was nearly 10:00 p.m.

Maybe he'd gone to Baton Rouge. Maybe he had a girlfriend.

Maybe she should have her head examined.

He nodded. "Mama's Cajun Kitchen," he told her between bites.

Mama's was a relatively new place out on the highway toward Baton Rouge. Most of its customers were travelers passing through or staying at the newer motels. And since a rave review in the city newspaper, people actually drove out from Baton Rouge just to eat at Mama's.

Bryn figured Cole would know that. And as intense as he could be, even he needed a break from the thing that was taking over their lives. The past.

"Then I drove around for a while," he added. "Tried to find a few of the people on my list."

He'd obviously meant it when he'd said he wasn't going to be wasting a minute of these two weeks. "Did you?" she asked.

Cole shook his head. "The Fleur de Lis was closed. I tried Erica Saville's home address but she wasn't there either. I tried a couple of other addresses I'd found in the directory, but no luck."

"It's Friday night. And the Zydeco Festival's going on. Lots of people are out."

"You're not," he pointed out. He took another bite of the cookie pie and watched her.

"Bellefleur's pretty much a twenty-four/seven kind of job," she told him. Not that she felt like partying anyway. "Some guests came in from Lake Charles for the weekend."

She'd hoped to fill up the plantation's rooms with Zydeco tourists, but it hadn't happened. She'd spent the evening analyzing promotion strategies to increase her business by the next local event. Trouble was, promotion cost money. After the couple from Lake Charles had dropped off their bags and taken off for their night on the town, she'd walked around the mansion wondering which treasured piece she was going to have to sell next. And whether it was all worth it. It had been a stressful day all around.

And she'd taken some of that stress out on Cole.

His chair scraped back, and she watched him walk

over to the sink and put his wrapper in the trash. He moved toward the hall, but turned back in the doorway.

All he had to do was look at her for her heart to flip-flop. His darkly brooding eyes held hers with all that mysterious intensity that so defined him.

And so confused her.

"You look tired, Bryn," he said softly. "Go to bed."

"I have guests," she said. "They'll need to be let in."

Cole had let himself in with his guest key, but for safety purposes she flipped the security lock at ten o'clock every night. Guests who came in later than that had to be let in and the mansion secured again. With the Zydeco Festival in play tonight, she could be up late.

He stood there for another long beat and she knew she should say more, wanted to say more...

"Good night, Bryn." He left.

Her insides twisted with a sense of urgency to make him understand her rudeness, forgive her. But the words to explain stopped in her throat and she let him walk away. Alone, she crumpled the cookie pie wrapper in a tight fist then tossed it on the table. The bulb over the sink chose that moment to snap.

The darkness felt thick with regret. New regret, old regret. It all swam together.

She went out of the kitchen, through the shadowed hall. Chandelier light flooded the entry, left on for her guests. She flipped the security lock and looked up the sweep of stairs. The click of Cole's door shutting came to her as she reached the steps. Without giving herself time to think, she ran up the staircase and headed straight for his room. Her knock sounded confident, but when he opened the door, she felt pure nerves.

"I'm sorry about snapping at you before the tea," she blurted out. "You were trying to help and I was rude."

She waited for him to say something, anything. Her chest felt tight, achy, needy. She didn't want to feel this way.

The beaded lamp in the sitting area backlit his face and his expression was hard to read or even see.

"You don't have to apologize," he said quietly. "I'd be an idiot if I didn't understand. I don't want to do anything that will interfere with your business. And I hope that's not why you were sitting down there eating fifty Moon Pies."

"Three," she corrected. "I only ate three. I was a little stressed out."

"There are better ways to relieve stress."

There was a sensual tease in his voice. Was he flirting with her? When was the last time a man had flirted with her? Or that *she'd* flirted with a man?

Reckless thoughts to be having as she stood here with Cole.

"I'm sorry. I'll let you get to bed." She turned away, but his strong hand appeared on her forearm, bringing her back.

"Hey." His eyes burned through the shadows. "Thank you."

God, she'd been nothing but rude to him since he'd arrived at Bellefleur and now he was being *nice*. She felt so, so small.

"I was wrong, that's all, and—" And what? Her emotions were a jumbled wreck right now. She couldn't bear to meet his eyes.

"And you're stressed," he finished for her.

She lifted her eyes. He was so damn dangerous to her pulse. He'd let go of her arm, but he still stood there, so close, so incredibly, heart-stoppingly gorgeous, and if she had a brain in her head she'd already be halfway to her own room.

"I've got something for that," he said.

Her heart all but jumped out of her chest before she realized he was turning away to pour her a glass of merlot from the low table in the sitting area. Beyond lay the rosewood half-tester bed, piled high with a down comforter, blankets and pillows. An antiqued white nightstand, its curvaceous lines picked out in gold leaf, sat beside it. Cole's watch and a pair of eyeglasses rested on a pile of papers. He wore glasses to read, she realized with a jolt. The vision of Cole in those eyeglasses came to her as startlingly sexy.

It was all too intimate and unnerving. She was in his bedroom now, learning things about him she didn't want to know. He was a stranger and she should keep it that way.

And yet somewhere inside her, she knew he was no stranger at all and she didn't want to leave. She wanted to know the man who had grown out of the boy she'd loved. It was crazy and awful but unbearably true.

"I can't—" she started, but he said, "You can," and he pressed the glass into her hand.

It would be ungracious to hand it back, to run. Or maybe she just didn't want to do either of those things.

"You can sit down," he said, and there was a twitch of amusement curving his hard lips. "You can relax. You don't have to be on duty twenty-four/seven, Bryn. It's not good for you. Take a break. Smell the roses."

She almost choked on the sip of wine she'd taken. "Right. And I bet you do that." Mr. Hotshot Attorney.

He looked up from pouring his own glass. "I do when I need to." He came back toward her and took her hand. She was too surprised to stop him when he led her to one of the upholstered chintz chairs. She perched on the seat, as if sitting back would be too huge a commitment. He sat down in the other chair, stretched his long, jean-clad legs. "I drove down to the bayou this evening and just walked around."

"You're comparing smelling the roses to hanging out with alligators?"

He laughed. "Nothing like the scent of wild muscadine and the feel of marsh grass under my feet to remind me who I am. We lived off the swamps when I was a kid. Between plantation jobs, we'd camp out, live out of our pickup, and cook crawfish and rice over an open fire. We knew how to survive. It wasn't all bad, though. Those were some of the best times of my life."

The spooky realm of the slow-moving bayous had never appealed to Bryn. "I was always afraid of swamp monsters."

"The monsters aren't in the swamps, Bryn."

The clock on the bed stand across the room ticked in the silence. The window was open, and the heavy breeze sighed in the oaks outside.

"You never told me about living off the swamps," she said finally.

"I didn't think talking about living out of a pickup and eating crawfish by the bayou was going to impress a girl who'd grown up at Bellefleur."

"Were you trying to impress me?"

"Of course."

Damn his lazy charm. She took another sip of the merlot. He looked so relaxed, and she was so…not. "You could have told me some lies about wrestling eight-foot alligators."

"Would that have impressed you?"

"I was always impressed with you, Cole." Her hazardous admission hung in the humid air between them. But there were things she hadn't said fifteen years ago and she owed it to him to say them now. "I always knew you'd be a success. I wasn't surprised to see how far you've come. I'd never met anyone like you. You didn't have rules and boundaries. You made me think I could live that way, too."

It was an uncomfortable, scary thought. Her life had always run on some track that had been laid down before she was born, and Cole had made her imagine living outside of that track.

"Your father would never have let us be together," he pointed out, and something grim entered his voice.

She wanted to tell him he was wrong, but she knew better. At sixteen, she'd looked at life through rose-colored glasses. She'd thought dreams really did come true. But even if Aimee hadn't died, her father still wouldn't have given his blessing for her to be with Cole. And she probably wouldn't have had the courage to openly rebel.

"My father had some outdated ideas about proper debutante behavior. He was going to throw a ball for us that summer."

"A ball. Like with ballgowns and Scarlett O'Hara dancing?"

He almost got her to smile. "Hey, it's tradition. That's why we were taking dance that summer." Then… "It never happened."

"I never thought about how much your life must have changed after Aimee died," he said quietly. "Not till I came here and saw you again."

"I lost everyone."

"You've still got your mom."

Emotion pricked behind her eyes. "She can't help you find any answers about Aimee, Cole."

A taut beat stretched, then, "Why not?"

He didn't sound angry, but he deserved an answer. "My mother had a series of small strokes a few years ago." She worked to make her voice steady, mechanical. "As a result, she suffered what's known as vascular dementia. It's caused by an extensive narrowing of the arteries and blood supply to the brain. She has trouble thinking, reasoning, remembering. Sometimes she doesn't know who I am."

Her throat was damnably thick now.

"At first we thought she might have Alzheimer's," she went on, "and she went through a lot of testing before they figured it out. She's being treated, but it's irreversible and it will only get worse. Not many people know about her condition. She was depressed for a long time after Aimee died, so she'd pretty much withdrawn from any type of social life. She lives in one of the cottages on the grounds with a nurse."

"I'm sorry about your mother, Bryn." The sympathy shining in Cole's eyes threatened to break her control.

"You know what's ironic? My mother is pretty happy now. Most of the time, she either can't remember Aimee at all or she can't remember that she died." If only she could forget, too. "Mr. Brouchard keeps camellias all around the cottage for her. They were always her favorite flowers. All it takes to make her happy now is a camellia."

Her voice wobbled and she stopped to clear her throat. "I have to go now." Her chest hurt, and stupid tears were scorching hot and traitorous behind her eyes. She could *not* fall apart in front of Cole.

She got up, ready to run.

She'd taken only a few steps when she realized the glass of merlot was still in her hand. She turned, meaning to set it down, but he was there. She bumped into him and the merlot sloshed everywhere—his shirt, her top, the heart pine floor. That was going to make a stain if she didn't get it up.

"I'm sorry," she said roughly. There were napkins somewhere. The table. She tried to push past him blindly but he wouldn't let her.

"Bryn."

He was in her way, all six brooding feet of him.

"I'll clean it up," she said.

"Forget it, it's nothing. It's you I'm worried about." He reached out, touched her arm.

"I'm fine," she said desperately. "I'm worried about the floor. I can't afford to have it refinished if that makes a stain." Then that was it, she was crying like a baby. Over a floor.

She pushed past him and this time she made it to the stack of napkins on the table. She knelt on the floor, and damn him, he was right there, helping her. They sopped up the wine and she tried to stop crying but it was as if she'd opened some floodgate and couldn't shut it back. He didn't say anything, just wiped up the floor, then took her hand and lifted her to her feet.

"I'm sorry," she whispered after she'd put the wet napkins in the trash. She just needed to get the heck out of Dodge, and yet leaving was the last thing she wanted to do. It was nonsensical and frightening, and yet still she didn't move. "I'm just a little stressed about money right now and—" She squeezed her eyes shut against the unbearable compassion in his gaze.

"You're not crying about the floor, Bryn." She felt him thumb away one of the hot tears on her cheek, then he pulled her into his arms. "You're doing too much and you're doing it alone."

He was right, she wasn't crying about the floor. It was all the intense feelings of the past few days, spinning together in one huge maelstrom of emotion. He was stroking her back soothingly, and it was comfort, nothing but comfort. Then she opened her eyes and saw the truth beyond the controlled consolation of his embrace.

A truth that crackled between them as if it were alive. He wasn't touching her any differently, but it suddenly seemed shockingly intimate.

All her aching need was his aching need, too. All the pain, all the heartache, all the guilt, they'd shared it all along. They'd both lost so much. And tonight, the things that had torn them apart didn't seem to matter as much as what pulled them together.

Her room seemed far away and utterly lonely and she knew why she didn't want to leave. And if she was kidding herself about why she was going to stay, she didn't want to know.

"Maybe you should go," he said, and there was a shake to his voice. "Because I'm—"

"I don't want—"

"—not sure I can handle it if you don't."

"—to be alone."

"Bryn—"

She kissed him.

Chapter 10

Cole closed his eyes, dizzy with pleasure at the sensation of Bryn's tongue sweeping inside his mouth, sweetly, delicately, claiming his sanity. This was wrong, so wrong, had to be wrong. But he'd longed for her from the instant he'd laid eyes on her again at Bellefleur.

Hell, *before* he came back to Bellefleur. And he couldn't remember why this was so wrong....

His fingers were running through her hair, down her back, and she was kissing him as if she couldn't get enough of him. Her body pressed against him, setting off shockwaves of desire inside him. Hunger and passion and hope were all there for the taking, and he took it, pulled her up into his arms, carried her to the half-tester bed in two long strides, then strode back long enough to kick the door shut. And he stood there, barely breathing, the bang of his heart against the wall of his chest hurting him. Everything inside him hurt. And she was hurting, too. She sat there on the bed, staring up at him with desperate eyes, wide and haunted and wet.

"Bryn—"

"I don't want to be alone," she said again, this time in a broken whisper. "I need this tonight."

She needed *this*. Not him. *This*. But when she reached for him, there was no way he wasn't going to respond. He had to kiss her again or everything inside him was going to tear apart. He tumbled back onto the bed with her and when he kissed her, he didn't hurt anymore. He didn't feel pulled thin by grief or on fire from bitterness.

Her hands skimmed down his back, dragging him closer, and nothing else existed. Just her mouth and her hands and her low, unbearably sexy moan as he slipped his hand between them and touched her breast through her shirt. She pulled away just long enough to grab the hem of her T-shirt and pull it over her head, then greedily, needily, her mouth claimed him again. He could feel her naked breasts pushing against his chest and he was nearly mindless.

He slipped beside her, pulling her over top of him. Her eyes were close, softly shining in the low lamplight, and she was more beautiful than he could believe. Her mouth was full and wet and her hands…her hands were tearing apart the clasp of his pants. He'd never wanted any woman this way before, and as she tugged down the zipper on his jeans, he was instantly, totally, frenetically lost. She reached for his shirt now, and he helped her tear it off.

Then she pulled off him and he could have died before he realized she'd stood to draw off her shorts. She stood there, naked but for sheer black panties, all silvery smooth skin and big, aching eyes, like a dream, a ghost, but when she came back to him, sweeping off his jeans and underwear, so bold and ravenous, she was no ghost, no dream, she was real. They fell back onto the bed again and he gave in to her, ravaging her with his mouth, his teeth. His hands possessed her and he was shocked at the strength of the need they shared. He shifted her to his side, pulled over her and forced himself to slow down, tear his mouth off hers, when all he wanted was more and more.

The smell of her hair, the taste of her lips, the feel of her unbelievable—naked—body. More, more, more.

More Bryn.

Somewhere very far in the back of his consciousness the word *wrong* came back and he knew he should say something, remind her why they shouldn't do this, but emotion filled his throat and blood drummed in his head.

She watched him in that long, tender moment and then she reached between them and touched him. He was so far gone, beyond lost, on some other planet where Bryn and this bonfire she'd started in his veins were all that mattered. He trailed scorching kisses down her throat, taking her breasts in each hand, tracing circles around her taut peaks with his tongue. She moved restlessly, urgently against him, and his hands caressed their way lower, sliding inside the sheer panties to cup her hot, damp core, then thrusting inside. She urged him on, grinding her hips to push herself into his palm, gasping as he stroked her. Her head fell back against the bed and she sighed raggedly, rocking into him. Then she slayed him by coming in soft, remarkable shudders, responding instantly to his touch, a cry sliding out of her mouth that he swallowed with a kiss.

Heart thundering, he took in her flushed face, tangled, damp hair, and wide, hungry eyes, was nearly undone when she encircled again his own hot, desperate need. She pulled him into her, wrapping her legs around him, gripping him so tightly. She kissed him again, hard, and he drove inside her, not about to deny her anything. She was slick and ready and not stopping.

She rocked beneath him and heat sang in his blood. Her legs and arms grasped him wildly, not letting him slow down, demanding more, and when she shuddered in his arms again, he could no longer think at all. His body drove into her one last time as he followed her into that perfect, sweet oblivion.

He lay there with her, eyes closed, feeling as if his cellular structure had been fragmented and he was left limp and lost and trembling. Bryn lay beneath him, her breaths quick against his skin, her arms still clinging to him as if he were her lifeline. He didn't want her ever to stop clinging to him, and that scared him to death. He couldn't stop thinking. He knew, he just knew, she was going to regret this.

And he knew he wasn't.

The distant, insistent chime from the front door broke through the whispery heaviness of the house. It took a Herculean effort for Bryn to move her sated, heavy limbs. She didn't want to move.

She rolled away from Cole, and his arms pulled her back.

"Bryn, wait."

If she turned, if she looked at him right now, she'd never be able to do what she had to do. Get up. Go. Get on with her life. What they'd just done hadn't changed anything. It had been sex, just sex. A release from all the tension.

"I have to go," she said quietly. "I have guests. The security lock is switched. I have to let them in." That she had even done this stupid thing when she had guests returning any minute rubbed in the sheer power she'd let Cole have over her senses.

She got up, cold, shivering, and she told herself not to think about being naked. So she was naked. So was he. She had all the same body parts as any other woman, and hell, he'd seen her naked before. It was no big deal. She pulled on her clothes with shaking, weak fingers, her body still in some kind of trembling aftermath of extremely powerful sex. Cole. She'd had sex with Cole. She'd gone stark, raving, straitjacket mad.

And it *was* a big deal. She didn't jump in the sack on a casual basis. That wasn't her. Frankly, she didn't jump in the sack at all. She'd had a few hopeless relationships in college, then her father's death and Bellefleur had taken over her life. And she'd settled for a comfortable friendship with Drake. Then Cole had come back and it had taken her just over twenty-four hours to take up where they'd left off. They hadn't even used protection, she realized with a jolt. Her impetuous stupidity around Cole knew no bounds.

What did that say about her real feelings for him? She didn't want to know. It was more than she could handle.

He'd taken away the pain, the grief, the awful aching emptiness, that had to be all it was. And she couldn't blame him for anything. It had been her, all her, who had made it happen. A result of all the high emotions that had been tearing her apart. And it had been all too easy to forget herself in Cole's arms.

She couldn't let it happen again.

"Don't run away from this, Bryn." His voice came

low and harsh as she reached the door. And close. Too close.

His hand clamped down on hers as she reached for the doorknob.

Cole had pulled on his pants, but that was all. In the lamplight, he looked gorgeous in that brooding way of his.

"I'm not running," she lied desperately.

His eyes were hot on hers. "Looks like running to me."

"I have to go. I have to let my guests in."

"We need to talk."

"No, we don't." Somehow, her voice actually sounded normal.

"What just happened here then?" His voice, however, didn't sound normal. It sounded hard, and maybe even hurt. But surely she was imagining that.

"Stress relief," she said coolly despite the tightening in her throat. "Or a trip down memory lane. Call it whatever you want." It was incredibly complicated. "Let's not make a big deal out of this."

The doorbell chimed again.

"Please, I have to go." She pulled away from him and this time he didn't stop her. She ran down the stairs to the bright-lit foyer and faced her returning guests who were full of questions about things to do and see the next day around St. Salome Parish. When they went finally up to bed, she saw that Cole's door was shut. Thank God. She was alone again, and she would deal with this stupid thing she'd done. She would be fine. She took a shower and put on a long T-shirt for bed.

In the French-carved frame of her gilded mirror, she took in the haunted darkness of her eyes against her pale complexion. Despite the shower, she could still feel and taste and smell Cole, as if he were somehow imbued into her skin. She reached for one of the perfume bottles that marched across the dresser top and spritzed her neck. She picked up the hairbrush that lay in front of a canning jar filled with wildflowers and tore it through her still-damp hair as if that would remove the memory of Cole's fingers tangling there.

Hopeless, all of it.

She returned to her bed, flipped off the lamp that fought for space with a towering pile of favorite books. In the enfolding gloam of her lonely room, her body craved him. Her nipples throbbed, her mouth dried, her arms felt empty and yearning. She still wasn't fine—far from it—and she didn't know if she'd ever be fine again.

The ring of the telephone broke the fullness of the quiet night. Stumbling from bed, she made her to way to the desk in the office of her suite.

"Hello?"

"Bryn, it's me. I hope I'm not calling too late. I just got in from dinner."

Drake. Her chest constricted. "I'm still awake." She sat down behind the desk.

"I wanted to check on you. Make sure you're all right."

She knew what he was really worried about. Cole. Drake of all people knew how hard this investigation into Aimee's death would be for her. And even though she'd told him there could be nothing but friendship between them, he'd still called. He still cared.

"I'm all right," she said softly.

"I've been thinking about it," Drake said, and he didn't have to define *it*. "I know you agreed to help him. I know that you can't bear the idea that someone could still be walking free who killed Aimee, but you know it's not true. I called that Blue Water Shores place in Tampa. They've never heard of Randol Ormond."

Bryn blinked. "What? That's impossible. Cole—"

"Exactly. This whole thing is impossible, Bryn. Cole's lying. He's not here for the truth. He's here for revenge."

"Maybe there was a mistake."

"Or maybe he's a liar."

She swallowed thickly. Her mind swam with disbelief. "I'll talk to Cole about it in the morning. Maybe he has an explanation."

Drake was silent for a beat. "Bryn, I don't want you there with him. Come to Baton Rouge. You can stay in my apartment."

"You know I can't do that. There's Bellefleur. I have guests tonight. This is Zydeco weekend—"

"Damn Bellefleur." His voice heated. "That place is killing you, Bryn. Marry me. Forget Bellefleur. Forget the bed and breakfast. I need you here. I want you to be my wife."

A band of sadness seized her heart.

"I told you I can't marry you," she whispered into the phone.

"Bryn—" There was pain in his voice. "I'm sorry. I blew my cool for a second." She could feel him through the phone, across the miles, regaining his control. "I'm sorry. If you need more time, take it. I'm just worried about you."

"More time won't change anything," she told him shakily.

"I don't want to lose you, Bryn."

"I'm sorry." The catch in her voice made it hard to go on. "You've always been there for me and I love you for that, but I can't marry you. It wouldn't be right. I don't feel for you the way I should feel for someone… Someone I could marry." The starkness of the admission made her stomach sick. She didn't want to hurt Drake. She wanted them still to be friends, but maybe that was a pipe dream. His feelings were even stronger than she'd realized. "Time isn't going to change how I feel."

"Is this about Cole?"

She squeezed her eyes shut for a painful beat. "It's about me, Drake." She apologized again, but this time he didn't say anything. "I'll call you if I find out anything about Randol Ormond."

After she'd said goodbye and hung up, she sat there for the longest time. Could her night get any worse? She'd made love with Cole, then she'd hurt the one person who's supported her all these years and it was no comfort that it had been the right thing to do. She had to be firm. She couldn't do anything to lead him on. But it still wounded her.

The phone rang again before she left the desk.

"Hello?"

A gravelly whisper crept through the phone line, "Is Aimee there?"

Chapter 11

She didn't move, couldn't move, for a horrible pulse-beat, then she slammed the receiver down. The telephone rang again immediately.

The line ached in awful silence when she picked it up.

"Is this Aimee?"

"Who is this?" Bryn demanded shakily. There was no answer. "Stop calling here!"

She slammed the phone down again. And it rang.

Bryn grabbed the cord out of the wall. She lay down in bed again, her skin crawling. From all the way downstairs, she could hear the distant ring of her phone in the office on the first floor.

It stopped. And then it started again.

Bryn dragged a drawer open, banging it onto the floor with the strength of her pull, and stepped into a pair of shorts. She burst out of her room, raced down the stairs, her heart in her throat all the way. The office light blinded her when she flipped it on. The phone rang and rang.

She reached across the desk and grabbed the receiver.

The harsh whisper filled her ear. "Aimee?"

She heard footsteps pounding through the thick claw of anger and fear as she yanked that line from the wall, too. She turned, found Cole in the doorway. The sharp angles of the light revealed unreadable eyes.

"I heard you run out of your room," he said. "I just had to see if you were all right, after what happened last night."

The brick. Now these phone calls. Were they pranks, kids from town who knew the old, scary ghost stories of murder and had heard Cole was back? Or people in town who didn't like the revival of a horrific scandal, the mere whisper that someone else might have been responsible, one of them?

Or was Cole right? Was there a murderer stalking free in Azalea Bend? Someone who didn't like the fact that Cole was in town to find the truth about Aimee's death?

And could she trust anything Cole had told her about Aimee's murder? He stood there with his pierc-

ing, inscrutable eyes and she didn't know the answers
to any of her questions. She'd had sex with him and
the stark truth was, she really didn't know him.

Feeling overwhelmed, she struggled for a deep,
steadying breath. For a sliver of sanity in her upside-
down world.

All she really wanted to do was throw herself into
Cole's arms and let his warm, hard, dangerous body
make her forget all this devastation and heartache
again. But he was part of that devastation and heartache, and she couldn't trust him.

"It's just some prank phone calls," she told him,
amazed at how cool her voice sounded, as if she
weren't just about to crack. "Somebody asking for
Aimee."

Cole swore, and started to move toward her. She
stepped back, unsure if it was because she was afraid
of him or of herself.

He stopped abruptly, his expression tightening.
"Do you have caller ID?"

A bitter breath came from her throat. "You've got
to be kidding. I can't afford extras, Cole."

"Get it," he said. "Tomorrow. It's not an extra if
you're being harassed." He sounded angry and protective. She'd love nothing more than to feel as if he
could protect her, but she was beyond any ability to
know how to feel about Cole.

The shivery reminder of the passion they'd shared
throbbed low in her belly. Her body needled with an

almost excruciating desire even as her rational mind knew his intentions were still circumspect.

"There's no Randol Ormond at Blue Water Shores in Tampa," she said sharply. "Drake called there. They told him they'd never heard of Randol Ormond."

Cole's jaw tensed. "That's impossible. I went to Tampa and met with Randol Ormond in person, Bryn."

"Did you? How do I know? Where's Randol Ormond?"

Cole strode toward her and seized her shoulders with an insistent grip. "I don't know, Bryn. Maybe he got scared. Maybe someone threatened him. My father didn't kill Aimee—and that means someone else did. Maybe they went after Randol Ormond. You know I'm telling you the truth. You know it in your heart or you wouldn't be helping me and you wouldn't have—" He broke off, but he didn't have to finish.

She wouldn't have made love to him the way she had unless somewhere deep inside, she was starting to believe him. And she could be so wrong. She could be a complete fool.

"You don't know what I think or how I feel about anything!" She tore away from his intolerably electric hold.

She moved behind the desk, to a position of safety. Away from Cole, with the broad, polished desk buffering her from the desperate nearness of him. When she was close to him, she couldn't think or reason. She was more confused than ever about Aimee's death, and she had to keep this whole thing from driving her mad. She had Bellefleur. She had guests upstairs right now, dammit, and she was lucky they hadn't heard the commotion.

"I know one thing," he said, and something hard and hurting in his voice nearly broke her. "You want the truth about Aimee as much as I do."

She tipped her chin at Cole and mustered all the strength she had left in her. "The only thing I want right now is for you to leave me alone."

Cole did his best to keep out of Bryn's way for the remainder of the weekend. When he'd seen her the next morning, she'd looked pale and shaky, almost sick, and there had definitely been nothing welcoming about the look she'd given him. He knew she didn't want to see him. Hell, she'd *told* him she didn't want to see him. But in truth, that wasn't the only reason to put some distance between them. He didn't trust himself around her as far he could throw himself.

All he wanted every time he got near her was to pull her back into his arms and make mad, mindless love again. He wanted to rip her clothes off and claim her like a Neanderthal. He wanted her in his arms, in his bed, every night, and he wanted to make her admit that she wanted him, too.

But Bryn looked at him as if he was the embodiment of some new disease every time he saw her.

There was no way she was going to talk about what had happened—much less let it happen again.

As promised, she'd dug out the sugarcane records as well as the names of the yard boys the summer Aimee died. Her guests stayed all weekend, plus she had a number of visitors for the mansion tour. It all made it so much easier for her to act as if he were dead. Cole had plenty to keep him busy, and he'd begun to realize what a huge job he'd set himself. He'd contacted Ken Bryant, one of the firm's investigators in Baton Rouge, who was helping him track down some of the more elusive names on his list. He was also in the process of lining up an expert to examine the original forensic document. No way was he handing it over to any authorities in Azalea Bend without having it authenticated first by his own expert. St. Salome Parish had screwed this thing up fifteen years ago and he wasn't about to trust them now.

In the meantime, he'd started asking the questions nobody had asked fifteen years ago. His experience in the courtroom—along with his gut instinct—told him that Aimee, like most murder victims, had been killed by someone close to her—and there had been a reason, a very personal reason, someone had wanted her out of the way.

He tracked down Emile Brouchard at work on the front drive Saturday morning. The day was muggy and warm, even beneath the sheltering magnolias. The older man pulled down the protective mask shielding his mouth and nose from the insecticide he'd been spraying on the trees when Cole approached. He nodded a wary greeting.

"I'd like to ask you a few questions about the summer Aimee Louvel died," Cole started.

The older man's eyes narrowed. "Miss Louvel doesn't need any trouble."

"I'm just asking questions. I'm not looking to cause trouble for Bryn."

Emile looked as though he doubted that statement. "What do you want to know? I've got work to do."

Cole showed him the list of yard boys he'd gotten from Bryn. "Did you ever see any of these boys with Aimee?"

"Mr. Louvel wouldn't have been allowing that," Emile said immediately.

Maurice Louvel wouldn't have allowed Bryn to see him either, so that didn't mean much to Cole, but if Aimee had been seeing any of the yard boys, apparently Mr. Brouchard hadn't known about it.

He tried a different tack.

"Were they good workers? Were any of them trouble?"

Emile shrugged. "Well, there was that Navin boy." He shot a thick, work-hardened finger at one of the names. "I remember him. He got in fights a lot. Sometimes he came to work beat up. Half the time he didn't show up."

"Did you see him the day after Aimee died?"

"Everybody was sent home from the Great House that day except the cook and Mathilde," Emile said. "The family was in mourning."

"What do you remember about the day of the murder?"

Brouchard scratched his head for a beat. Wind rustled through the magnolia leaves. "It was an unusually dry summer. We'd been fighting leaf scorch pretty bad. Lost a couple dogwoods, in fact. I remember talking about it to Mr. Louvel."

Cole worked on his patience. "What about Aimee? Did she seem happy, distracted, worried about anything?"

"I don't remember even seeing her that day." Emile shook his head. "Might have seen her. Might not. It was a long time ago."

"Can you think of anyone who might have had a motive to hurt Aimee Louvel?"

"Wade Dempsey."

Cole's chest twisted at the flat response.

Emile Brouchard pulled his mask back up, tugged the elastic band around his head again. He was done with the conversation. He picked up the sprayer. "You don't want to be standing in line with the breeze when I'm spraying," he said through the mask, then turned back to his work.

The wagons were as tightly circled as ever around the Louvels.

Emile Brouchard and his sister Mathilde still lived

in one of cottages on plantation property. It had been, Bryn had explained, granted to them for their lifetime by her father when he'd sold off most of the land, in appreciation for their family's generations of service to the Louvels.

Mathilde was a tiny scrap of a woman with a trapped-doe look in her eyes. She opened the door to Cole with evident reluctance.

"I wasn't at the Great House the day Aimee died," she told him when asked. "It was my day off." She sat on the cottage's olive-drab sofa with her ankles crossed, looking like a wrinkled little girl with her curly brown hair that sat somewhat askew on her small head, like an ill-fitting wig. If she remembered anything about Aimee's activities that summer, she wasn't offering it up, no matter how many different ways Cole posed his questions.

"What about the next day? Did you see anyone who appeared to have been in a fight? Someone with their face scratched, maybe."

Mathilde told him she couldn't remember anything and showed him the door.

Nellie Brewer, the Louvel cook, lived in a Cracker-jack-box-sized house in one of the older sections of Azalea Bend. He remembered her as a six-foot-tall hulk of a woman who'd ruled the Louvel kitchen like her own personal military camp. She was still tall, if thinner and frailer, but just as protective of the Louvels as ever when he interviewed her.

"It was just a normal day," the cook said.

The day Aimee died had apparently been the most ordinary day in Azalea Bend history. And Aimee Louvel had been the sweetest, purest angel who'd ever walked the earth. No one could have had a reason to kill her.

He called the Blue Water Shores several times and so far he hadn't gotten past the receptionist who claimed to have never heard of Randol Ormond. He'd left several messages for the director, but so far, no callback. Cole had put Bryant, his private investigator, on the trail of Ormond's family. Somebody somewhere knew where Randol Ormond had gone.

Meanwhile, he was hitting brick wall after brick wall as he continued down his list. He'd found an Edward Navin in the phone book and knocked on his door—and gotten it slammed in his face when he'd started asking questions about Tommy. He had a hot coil of frustration tightening his stomach by the evening he walked into the Fleur de Lis. Black-cherry potpourri assailed his nostrils as he entered the small downtown boutique. The shop was stuffed with everything from vintage clothing and custom jewelry pieces to dried flower arrangements and pottery. Erica Saville was an attractive woman with swingy chestnut hair and sharp topaz eyes.

He waited while she finished ringing up a couple of customers. It was closing time and she flipped the sign on the door as they left.

"I was wondering when you'd stop in here," she said. She leveled her tiger-on-the-prowl gaze on him and walked back toward him with a swing in her short-skirted hips. "I hear you're a big hotshot lawyer now. You sure grew up fine."

The way she was looking at him, he didn't think she was appreciating his jurisprudence degree.

"I'm looking into Aimee Louvel's murder."

"I heard that, too."

"You were taking dance with Bryn and Aimee that summer," he probed.

"I was." She stopped right in front of him and the heavy swirl of her perfume surrounded him.

"What do you remember about the day Aimee died?"

"I saw Bryn and Aimee at dance that day," she said. "It was a pretty normal day."

Again with the normal day. Cole's jaw tightened.

"Was Aimee upset or worried about anything?" He was grasping at straws, hoping against hope that eventually he was going to ask the right question to the right person.

Erica Saville studied him with her brazen eyes. "Take me out for a drink and I might think of something."

Chapter 12

Somebody was pissed off.

Cole came out of his bedroom the next morning and headed down the stairs in the direction of the cursing. Morning light rayed into the entry hall of Bellefleur. Sun motes pirouetted up the stairs to meet him along with some really bad words he didn't think Bryn had learned at ballroom-dancing lessons.

The front door was open, Bryn's curvy little body, all tight and cute in cut-off shorts and another one of her damnably sexy tops, caught his attention as she angrily swept at something, her back to him.

She'd been locked up in her office when he'd come back the night before. He hadn't told her about his conversation with Erica Saville yet. And he wasn't looking forward to it.

"You got that broom registered as a lethal weapon?" he asked calmly.

She whipped around. It was early, but already warm and sticky. Her face was flushed from exertion, making her blue-violet eyes brighter. The wild light in them reminded him of something else about water hyacinths—they were almost impossible to control. She flung the broom down.

"Look." She waved around, and stepped back.

And he saw it.

Some kind of red powder, everywhere, all over the portico and down the steps. And a big ugly chicken bone nailed to the front door with a piece of narrow wire.

There was a hammer on the porch floor, as if it had been flung there. Probably by Bryn.

"It's nailed in good," she bit out. "I could go get some wire clippers, but I really want the nail out. They damaged the door, too. That's going to leave a hole."

"What the hell is this?" He couldn't believe what he was seeing.

"Voodoo. Hex. Spell. Curse. *Gris-gris*. Whatever you want to call it."

Grabbing the hammer up, she attacked the nail again, struggling to yank it out. "First the brick through the window—" She huffed as she worked at the nail. Hair wisped across her cheeks. "—then those lovely prank phone calls. Then Mrs. Guidry calls first thing this morning to tell me that she's thought it over and I can forget any more St. Salome Garden Club events. And, oh yeah, I can forget the Library Ladies luncheon she'd mentioned scheduling at Bellefleur, too."

She yanked back again and this time the nail came with her and she rocked backward from the recoil of the release. "—and now this," she finished, regaining her balance. The nail had dropped at her feet, along with the chicken bone. She swiped at the hair in her face, tangling it in the sweat beading on her forehead. "I've got people laying the *gris-gris* on me."

"Who's Mrs. Guidry?"

Bryn put the hammer down. Beyond her, he saw Emile Brouchard approaching the house from the direction of his cottage. "Somebody told her about Wade Dempsey's son staying at Bellefleur. The Guidrys are old friends of the Cavanaughs. Mr. Guidry shared offices with Hugh Cavanaugh before he became the prosecutor."

Enough said.

He'd expected the town to be against him. He hadn't expected the town to turn against Bryn, and so quickly and thoroughly. She was more than collateral damage this time. She was taking the brunt of the town's anger. The brick, the phone calls, the cancellations and now this. The town might still revere the Louvels but the resentment against Cole and his accusations was stronger. They were punishing Bryn for his presence at Bellefleur. He'd rocked the boat and let the chips fall. But he hadn't meant them to fall so solidly on Bryn.

Guilt speared Cole. He'd rolled into town like a selfish bastard and she was paying the price. "I wanted to shake things up. I didn't want to hurt your business. I didn't want to hurt you." And what he had to tell her about his conversation with Erica Saville was going to hurt her even more. "I have to talk to you about Aimee."

She stood there looking like the last thing she wanted to do was talk to him about anything.

Emile Brouchard reached the porch. His gaze took in the chicken bone attached to the wire still sitting on the porch floor and the red powder everywhere. He scraped a hand through his scrub-brush white hair and shook his head.

"Oh, Miss Louvel. You got the *gris-gris* laid on you."

"I'm not afraid of the *gris-gris*," Bryn said impatiently. "I noticed this morning that one of the live oaks lost a limb in that storm. It's down across the path to the river. I'd appreciate it if you'd get that taken care of first thing."

"Will do." Mr. Brouchard didn't move to do anything about the live oak situation. "You got to heed the *gris-gris*," he insisted.

"There's no such thing as *gris-gris*," she snapped.

Mr. Brouchard didn't look convinced. Like plenty of people in St. Salome Parish, he believed the *gris-gris* required action. Bryn had been crossed, and she needed to be uncrossed.

"You make your own luck," Bryn went on, seeming to work to soften her tone toward the grounds-keeper, "and there's no such thing as curses. This was a prank, a stupid prank." Somehow her justification that the recent disturbing events at Bellefleur were just a prank rang hollow. "I appreciate your concern, Mr. Brouchard, but I'm fine. I have some fresh muffins in the kitchen. Why don't you grab a couple before you go to work?"

"I can help," he said, not ready to give in. "Mathilde, she knows the ways to take off the curses."

Bryn blew out a frustrated breath. "No, thank you."

He seemed finally to accept he was being dismissed. He disappeared inside the house.

She turned back to Cole. "Spit it out. What do you want to tell me about Aimee?"

"This isn't something I can just spit out, Bryn. Let's go inside."

The look she gave him was more than tired. It was worn. He wanted to put his arms around her, tell her everything was going to be all right. But sparking in those worn eyes was anger, and he knew she'd sooner chop his hand off at the wrist than let him touch her. He'd been making headway on gaining her trust until Randol Ormond had disappeared.

She wasn't giving him an inch now. And she sure as hell wasn't going to risk being alone with him. Not after what had happened the last time.

The sound of the phone ringing blistered through the air. Bryn pushed past him and headed for her office.

He came into the office after her. Emile Brouchard stood in the entry with a muffin.

"Mathilde? What is it?" She was silent for a minute. "Why don't you come over this afternoon? We can talk then."

She hung up and glared at Cole. "What do you want?"

He glanced around. Mr. Brouchard still stood in the entry hall, watching Cole as if he was standing guard over Bryn. Cole gave him a long look and shut the door when he didn't move.

Bryn leveled him with an impatient stare when he turned back.

"I talked to Erica Saville last night," he said. "I know what Aimee did the afternoon of the day she died. She drove into town and met Erica Saville at Boudreaux's." Boudreaux's was a greasy hamburger place near the high school that served up anything fried.

"And?" Bryn prompted. She swiped a strand of hair out of her face.

"Aimee was upset. She was asking a lot of questions. Not the kind of questions Erica expected to hear from Aimee Louvel."

"Get to the point, Dempsey."

He knew what she was doing. She was putting every bit of distance she could between them. She wasn't even going to use his first name now.

"The kind of questions she was asking—" Damn, he didn't want to say it. But he had no choice. He laid it out. "She was asking the kind of questions that made Erica Saville think she was pregnant."

"No way." The reaction was immediate and swift and sure. If Bryn had looked tired before, there was nothing exhausted about her now. Her eyes alone could have burned Cole up on the spot. "Aimee didn't even have a boyfriend."

"You didn't spend as much time with her that summer as usual. Maybe you didn't know her as well as you thought you did." His words weren't making her any less furious. "She was asking Erica how to know if you were pregnant, what were the signs, the symptoms. How long it took till you'd start showing."

"She wasn't even friends with Erica Saville!" Bryn shot back. "Why would she go to her if she was pregnant?"

"Erica had had an abortion a few months earlier. Aimee knew about it."

"Everybody knew Erica Saville had been pregnant! She wasn't the kind of girl Aimee hung around with. Aimee didn't even like her. Erica was always in trouble at school, and honestly, I always thought she was mean and so did Aimee. This is crazy. If Aimee had been pregnant, the first person she would have told about it would have been me. And the last person would have been Erica Saville."

Her eyes were shooting flames but her skin was pale as ice. "Wouldn't the autopsy report show if she'd been pregnant?" Bryn demanded.

"A blood screening for pregnancy isn't part of a medical, legal autopsy. They'd be screening for chemical toxins. And the cause of death was clear—blunt trauma to the head. The physical examination cites nothing out of the ordinary other than that, but what if she was pregnant, Bryn? Don't you want to know? Are you sure Aimee would have told you?"

"I'm positive." But her voice trembled.

"What if it had something to do with her murder?"

The question hung in the sticky air between them.

"Drake was right all along." Bryn's voice was steady again, hard. "You're not here for justice. You're here for revenge. You're here to smear my family's name—my father's, now Aimee's. You think if you fling around enough dirt about my family that people will forget that your father was a crazy drunken murderer?"

Her bitter words scorched a hole in his chest even though he knew they came out of her confusion and pain. He was the messenger and she was ready to shoot him.

"You don't have to believe me," he said. "Talk to Erica Saville for yourself. If you didn't know Aimee was pregnant, what else didn't you know about what was going on in her life that summer, Bryn? My father didn't kill Aimee, no matter how convenient that would be for you and everyone else in this town. And if you don't give a rat's ass about my father, I can understand that. But you have to care about Aimee. Go get the truth for yourself. Go see Erica Saville."

Her hot, angry eyes went cold. "I want you out of Bellefleur today. Two weeks or not, your time is up."

Her piece of crap car wouldn't start.

She finally gave up trying to get the dead engine to turn over and barely resisted kicking the damn car after she slammed out of it.

Of course Cole was standing there, all hot and hard intensity in his unreadable eyes. He hadn't said a word to her after she'd ordered him out of Bellefleur.

"Take mine." Cole dug the keys out of his hip pocket. "I'll be packed when you get back."

She didn't want to take anything of his. He was crazy. Certifiable. Aimee couldn't have been pregnant. And even if she had been, what the hell could that have had to do with her murder? It didn't mean anything either way. There was no genuine forensic report, no confession by Randol Ormond. She couldn't believe anything Cole said anymore. He had his own agenda. Revenge.

And yet the whispering doubts wouldn't leave her alone. What if he *had* seen Randol Ormond? What if that forensic report was real, after all? What if someone had threatened Randol Ormond and that was why he'd disappeared? What if Wade Dempsey hadn't killed Aimee? If Aimee had been pregnant, had that had anything to do with her death?

What if the real murderer was still walking free?

It all sounded so insane.

She'd peeled out of Bellefleur like a bat out of hell, but the closer she got to Azalea Bend on the flat, empty highway, the more she let up on the gas. Her hands shook on the wheel of the smooth-as-butter Cobra as she half convinced herself to turn back. *Go get the truth for yourself.* The haunting doubts fought with her common sense and everything she'd believed for fifteen years.

It wasn't until she made it to the first stoplight into town that she realized she had no brakes.

They wouldn't let him see her. He wasn't family. He wasn't, honestly, anything to Bryn as far as the hospital staff was concerned. Cole was just a stranger, an outsider, who was ready to tear the building apart brick by brick if that's what it took to find out what had happened to Bryn.

The call had come into Bellefleur as he was packing his bags. The Cobra had slammed into a truck in the middle of an intersection. She was still alive and that was the sum total of the information he could get out of the hospital official who'd telephoned to notify Bryn's family.

Apparently Bryn was right about the fact that most people in Azalea Bend had no idea her mother had become mentally incapacitated.

Melodie had shown up at the mansion right after the call, and they'd raced to the St. Salome Parish Hospital in her little VW bug, guilt and a blinding panic killing him all the way. It had been his fault if Bryn had been speeding into town, distraught. Sprinting inside the cold, tomb-like hospital, he'd slammed to a stop at the emergency desk. And gotten nowhere. Melodie wasn't any more successful in prying details about Bryn's condition from the reception staff. She'd been talking almost nonstop about her final exams, Bellefleur, the new guy she'd met at the Zydeco Festival, and half a dozen other topics. He figured this was her way of keeping her mind off Bryn, but he was ready to strangle her by the time a white-coated physician with a perfectly-sculpted head of thick brown hair emerged from double steel doors.

Cole planted himself in front of the doctor. "Are you treating Bryn Louvel? Can I see her?"

"Are you family?" The doctor scraped him with a cautious gaze from beneath his dark brows. He looked young, maybe fresh out of medical school, and probably not from Azalea Bend. Maybe he was the only person in St. Salome Parish who didn't know the Louvels, but Cole wasn't chancing it.

Melodie came up beside him. "I'm one of Bryn's employees," she told the doctor.

"I'm a friend," Cole said. Hell, he wasn't even that, but it was only a little lie. He just had to know that she was going to be okay. "Look, I'm not family. But I care about Bryn. I just want to know if she's all right." Every horrible injury possible had raged through his mind since that call had come in.

Maybe it was the infinitesimal break in his voice, but the young physician's formal posture softened just a notch and he took pity on him. He looked at Melodie, then back at Cole.

"She was real lucky she had an airbag. She's got some bruised ribs and shoulders, and she's in some pain. But she's going to be fine."

A two-ton load fell off Cole's shoulders. "Thank you." His knees felt weak, he was so relieved. "Can I see her?"

The doctor's empathy was apparently all used up. He shook his head. "Not now. But we'll be discharging her in about thirty minutes. She'll need someone to drive her home."

Cole would have liked to barge through those steel doors right then and there and find Bryn. But he had no doubt that would result in him being tossed out on his ear. He'd have to be patient. And he needed a car.

Melodie offered to drive Bryn home.

"You've got a final exam in a couple of hours," he reminded her. "Go ahead. I'll make sure Bryn gets home."

He'd noticed a car rental business near the hospital when he'd been driving around Azalea Bend over the weekend. It was within walking distance, and he'd had all of Melodie he could take. He convinced her he didn't need a ride.

He was leaving the hospital when he noticed a police officer pushing through the bank of glass doors. He recognized Martin Bouvier, the officer who'd responded to Bryn's call the night Cole had arrived at Bellefleur.

He turned around and followed Bouvier back inside.

"Excuse me," he said, catching up to the cop. "Bryn was driving my car when she had the accident. Can you tell me how I can find out where it is?" He didn't care if it was totaled. Bryn was alive and she was going to be all right. Nothing else mattered.

Martin Bouvier stopped. His level cop's eyes squared on Cole as he turned. "We're holding the vehicle in evidence," he said.

Cole did a double take. "Why?"

"Miss Louvel was conscious at the scene," Bouvier said. "She was able to tell the responding officer that the brakes failed. We had it checked out. The brake lines were cut."

Chapter 13

The glaring Louisiana sun highlighted the hollow-
ness of Bryn's eyes as she walked out of the hospital
to the medium-sized sedan Cole had rented. She
moved stiffly, and he could see she was still hurting.
He shut the car door after Bryn eased into the passenger seat of the sedan. He'd had the car running in
the soupy heat outside the emergency entrance to get
the interior cooled off for her.

The blow of the air conditioner filled the silence
after he sat down on the driver's side and closed his
door. He made no move to pull away from the curb.

Just looking at her made him feel as though he
wanted to do something he couldn't remember

doing since his father had been killed. He wanted to cry.

She could have died, and it would have been his fault. Since he'd found out about the cut brake lines, he'd been so angry he felt as if he might self-combust. This crash had been meant for him, only Bryn had been hurt instead. She looked like hell now. Her head rested back against the seat as if it was almost too heavy for her to support.

And she was lucky—lucky!—it hadn't been worse. If she'd been driving faster, if there hadn't been an airbag…

He felt a violent impulse to take revenge for what had happened, and yet with it came the chilling helplessness that he had no idea who was responsible.

"I knew you'd be here," she said quietly, staring out the window at the hospital.

"Why didn't you call someone?" She had to have a dozen friends she could have phoned. Drake Cavanaugh. Even Emile or Mathilde.

She turned her lovely, hurting eyes to him. "I don't know who to trust. I'm scared."

And she'd turned to him.

He knew a possessive, marrow-deep need to put his arms around her, as if that would keep her safe. He clenched his fists to keep himself from reaching for her. He had no right to hold Bryn in his arms, especially now. He was the one who had put her in this danger.

"This was my fault, Bryn. Someone cut my brake lines. It wasn't intended for you—it was meant for me."

"No, it's not your fault," she said, her voice low and angry through the bone-weariness. "I didn't know what to think all this time. Randol Ormond disappeared. I was so confused. And there were all those pranks. But this isn't a prank. Someone tried to kill you." Her eyes shone with an awful clarity. "Aimee's killer is still out there. Why else would someone have cut your brake lines?"

He shook his head. "I can't think of one other reason."

"No telling what happened to Randol Ormond," she whispered.

Guilt didn't even come close to describing how he felt. "I never meant for anyone to be hurt, Bryn. I just wanted to clear my father's name." For the first time he wondered if it was worth it. But at the same time, if he'd ever had a doubt about Aimee's murder, it had disappeared when Martin Bouvier had told him the Cobra's brake lines had been cut.

Someone wanted him dead. Someone was afraid of the questions he was asking, the doubts he was raising.

"We can't stop," Bryn said, and her voice broke. "We have to find the truth now."

"Not we, Bryn," he said immediately. "Me. You can't be part of this. Not anymore. That crash was meant for me."

"Aimee was my sister," she cried, then paused to draw a shaky breath. "I've already asked Martin to speak to the police chief for me, set up a meeting for tomorrow. I'm going to ask him to re-open the investigation into Aimee's death. And I've been thinking— we could contact the media. Get somebody interested, somebody from the Baton Rouge press, or even one of those national cable networks that showcase unsolved crimes. We could show them the forensic report. It's worth a try."

Cole felt a sick burning in his gut. She couldn't know what she was saying. "Bryn, I know we need help. I've got a private investigator on the case already. But if you put this in the hands of the police or the media right now, it's going to be out of your control and you don't know what will come of it. Who knows what else might come out?"

Already there was the possibility that Aimee had been pregnant.

"I don't care what comes out. Not anymore." Her hoarse voice was desperate, but he knew that deadly resolve in her anguished eyes. It was the same resolve that had brought him to Azalea Bend. "Somebody killed Aimee and they've been walking free for fifteen years. I can't live with that. I'm going to tell the police tomorrow that I want Aimee's body exhumed."

The sick burn crawled up his throat. "Bryn—"

"I'm going to close Bellefleur," she cut in, and the horrible catch in her voice tore at his heart. "I can't let guests stay there when—" She blinked back tears and looked away for an aching beat.

Someone had come onto the plantation in the night and cut his brake lines. The killer had been that close. There was no way she could keep the bed and breakfast open under those circumstances.

And all he could think was that she was putting herself straight in the bull's eye. No matter how much he wanted to clear his father's name, putting Bryn's life at risk had never been part of the equation. He'd known sheer terror such as he'd never known before when that call had come in from the hospital.

"I want you safe, Bryn. I want you out of this investigation."

She leveled her tormented gaze on him again. "You're not calling the shots, Cole."

He drove her back to Bellefleur. Bryn felt as if she could drop where she stood when she got out of the car, but her pain and exhaustion wasn't stopping her. She cancelled the few bookings she had coming up for the bed and breakfast, and Cole put a sign on the door suspending mansion tours. She called Melodie and let her know she wouldn't need to come into work, and punched in the number for Emile and Mathilde's cottage. Bellefleur was closed for business.

Fear licked her stomach with every passing moment, but her will to find the truth kept her going. She couldn't stop thinking about Aimee. The dark crush of knowing that her sister's killer had been walking free for fifteen years was beyond bearing. That, along with the fact that she now believed her father had killed Cole's for something he'd never done, was tearing her apart.

It was her father who'd been a murderer, not Wade Dempsey. The awful morass of that night got worse all the time and her emotions felt pulled on a thin, agonizing thread that could snap at any time.

"Brouchard."

"Mr. Brouchard, this is Bryn." Briefly, she told him about the accident. She didn't mention that the brake lines had been cut. No sense worrying him more than necessary.

"Are you all right?" Concern threaded his gruff voice.

"I'm fine. I'm home." She explained that the mansion was going to be closed, and rushed on before he could give her another lecture about the *gris-gris* or Cole or anything else. She was so tired. "Is Mathilde there? Will you let her know?"

"She's gone to cousin Georgitte's in Monroe," he said. "She'll be relieved to know you don't need her. Georgitte broke her hip. She might have to stay a while. She was real fretful about having to leave you."

Now she knew what Mathilde had wanted to discuss with her. She'd completely forgotten she'd told Mathilde to meet her at the house. "Tell her it's okay. I don't think I'll be opening Bellefleur any time soon."

She put down the phone after she'd told Emile

goodbye. Her head felt thick and heavy, as if it might fall off, and a nauseated lightness reminded her she hadn't eaten all day.

"Bryn, you've got to lie down," Cole said, coming into the office. He looked sick with worry. She wanted nothing more than for him to come over and put his arms around her, no matter how dangerous that would be. In her world gone mad, Cole had suddenly become safe. How crazy was that?

She straightened in her chair and winced from the bruising her body had taken when she'd been hit by the airbag in the crash.

"I'm going to lie down in a minute. I was just going to phone Emmie, check on my mom."

"What you need to do is call someone who can come stay with you," he said, and a strain entered his voice. "I'm not leaving you here alone."

She'd kicked him out. She'd forgotten that, too.

She started to shake her head, but nausea swam through her at the too-sudden movement. Her eyelids squeezed briefly against the sharp spear of pain. She was aware of Cole coming around the desk.

"God, Bryn, you're white as a sheet." His powerful arms enveloped her. "You're one sick puppy whether you want to admit it or not. You can call from upstairs." He helped her up and supported her up the steps. Her legs felt positively rubbery, but the way her pulse was tripping, it was more than the accident that was responsible for her reaction.

Cole was right about one thing, she was one sick puppy. As in demented with this need for him that no amount of common sense could assuage. When they reached her room, he pulled the sheets down on her bed while she changed into light pajamas in the bathroom, then he tucked her in like a two-year-old, and all the while her traitorous body yearned for him to lie down beside her and touch her as though she was anything but two years old.

He brought the phone in from the office in her suite and plugged it in to a closer outlet so she could have it by the bed.

He sat beside her. "I've already made arrangements to check in at the Bayou Star Inn on Route 43," he said grimly. "And you have my cell number if you need me. But you can't stay here alone. It's not safe. Either you call someone else, Cavanaugh even, or I'm staying."

A haunting quiet stretched between them. Shadows angled across Cole's hard features. He hadn't said a word damning her or her father since he'd picked her up at the hospital. He wasn't blaming her and his kindness was almost harder to bear than the anger with which he'd arrived at Bellefleur that first night.

But in that kindness, she saw again the tender boy of his youth. And all she wanted tonight was to hang on to that one tender thing left in her life.

"I don't want to call Drake," she said. "He's a friend, a good one, but I don't want a friend tonight."

Pausing, she took a deep breath.

"I want *you* to stay."

Somehow, he'd managed not to lie down on that bed with her. Somehow, he'd managed not to hold her and kiss her and oh, about a thousand other things he'd wanted to do.

Cole brought her a tray with a sandwich he'd fixed in the kitchen. No way was he leaving her alone, no matter how hard it was to stay. She was right—he wasn't her friend, and that she wanted more than a friend right now was killing him because that's what he wanted to be. Way more than a friend. But she was hurt, and he was trying his damnedest to do the right thing.

He hated to see the anguish shimmering in her eyes, hated even more knowing he'd set her down this terrifying, shattering path by his decision to come to Azalea Bend. He doubted she'd completely come to grips with it yet, but by accepting that Wade Dempsey hadn't killed Aimee, she'd accepted that her own father had murdered Cole's. He knew she wasn't ready to talk about it. The reality had to be too raw and awful.

And Cole was the one who'd brought all this grief and danger home to her. The truth about Aimee was coming with a terrible price tag already.

She'd insisted on taking a shower while he'd been getting her meal, despite the fact that she looked fragile as a strand of Spanish moss. She was way too stubborn for her own good. And for his. He'd found her coming out of the bathroom when he'd walked back into her room.

The image of her haunted him, the way she'd stood there wrapped only in a towel, the cotton sweeping low and barely covering her breasts. Her hair, dripping and tangled, and her big violet-smudged eyes made her look like a tragic nymph. He was all too human, and the soulful yearning uncloaked in that hurting gaze of hers in that unexpected moment had been almost more than he could take. He wanted her in this hot, blinding way that he didn't even understand, had given up understanding.

All his reasoning vanished every time he looked at her. He'd just stood there, every sense strangely heightened, and somehow he'd made his feet walk away.

He had to protect her from danger. Including the very real peril of him.

She slept the rest of the day while he made phone calls and paced and wanted to go outside and fight the phantom who'd cut those brake lines. In late afternoon, Emile Brouchard came out of one of the old barns riding a small tractor. Cole watched him from his window as he set about tearing up one of the overgrown gardens. Apparently, whether or not Bryn had the mansion open for business, Brouchard intended to continue keeping the grounds.

The sound of the machinery buzzed into the house,

but it didn't wake Bryn. It was nearly dark when he heard her come out of her room and pad down the stairs.

A wiser man would have stayed put, but he'd left wise behind a long time ago.

He followed her through the house, to the kitchen, where he found her standing in front of the refrigerator. The small fridge light illuminated her in its ghostly spill. The rest of the kitchen lay in the thin gloam of dusk.

She looked better, not so sick and frail as she had right after the accident. Her beautiful body was wrapped up in a thick robe, her feet bare. Her eyes were still vulnerable and hurting, and she just stared at him without saying a word.

Something inside his chest twisted when he thought of what could have happened to her in that crash, that she could be dead now instead of standing here so alive.

He went to her and cupped her face in his tender hands. "I haven't told you how glad I am that you're alive," he whispered hoarsely, and then there was no denying what he wanted to do. He kissed her.

Chapter 14

She kissed him back, sweetly, needily, and an instant rush of wonderful, hot sensations filled him. He felt his senses shred. This was everything that mattered. Bryn. In his arms. Alive. He had lost so many people in his life, and he couldn't bear to lose her. With a groan, he pulled her even closer, kissing her with all the aching, haunting passion inside he'd tried so hard to bury. He'd tried to convince himself this was just sexual attraction, pure need, but it wasn't true. It was the farthest thing from the truth.

The faint sound of the refrigerator door closing behind them brought him back to reality. He pulled away from her just enough to see her face in the dusky light that crept in through the kitchen window. Her eyes were huge, her lips wet, her skin opalescent. The violet smudges under her eyes remained.

He forced himself to let her go. She was exhausted, hurt. He couldn't claim her like the caveman she made him want to be.

"If you're hungry, I'll fix you something to eat," he said roughly. "You should go back to bed."

She shook her head. "I've had enough sleep. And I'm not really hungry. I'm restless, I guess." And yet she stood there, watching him with those soulful eyes. "Thank you for staying."

"I couldn't *not* stay, Bryn. I can't leave you alone."

"You make me feel safe," she said softly.

"I don't know if I can keep you safe," he told her, his chest crushed with the weight of his fear for her. "I'm sorry you're involved in this now. I'm sorry I ever came to Bellefleur and put you in this danger."

"I'm not sorry," she told him, and he could see the emotion shining in her damp eyes suddenly. "All this time, I never fought for Aimee. I believed everything I was told. I was wrong, and because of you, I have a chance to make it right."

"I don't want you to be hurt anymore." He couldn't bear the thought of anything else happening to Bryn.

"I don't care what happens," she said in a broken whisper. "As long as we find out what happened to Aimee, it's worth anything."

"It's not worth your life, Bryn." He couldn't help

it, he reached for her again, traced the pale line of her jaw. "I can't stand for anything else to happen to you. I nearly died inside when that call came in from the hospital." His voice shook.

"I should have believed you all along," she said, and her voice trembled, too. "I should have believed you fifteen years ago."

"You had no reason to believe me then," he said. "I pushed you too hard. I asked you to do something that would have hurt your family." He'd asked her to tell the police the truth about why his father had been fired. "It was too much to ask and it wouldn't have solved anything." He'd pushed her too hard since he'd come back, too.

"I was scared," she said in a small voice. "Maybe if I'd told the truth then, people would have asked more questions. Maybe the police would have looked harder into Aimee's death. Maybe—"

"Maybe doesn't matter now, Bryn." He couldn't stand to see her blame herself. After all these years, years in which he'd blamed Bryn, too, he knew it hadn't been her fault. He'd been hurt, bitter, and he'd blamed everyone. But he never should have blamed Bryn. He knew now how much she'd gone through, all the pain and grief that had seared these years for her. How her family had been destroyed as much as his own. "All that matters now is that you're not hurt again."

"I won't be. You're here."

Cole's heart clenched. He'd do anything for her. Anything. "I'm not going to let anything happen to you," he swore darkly. "If this madman, this killer, comes after you, he's going to have to get to you over my dead body. I'll sleep outside your door tonight if I have to."

"I don't want you to sleep outside my door."

Something taut hummed in the air. And her eyes locked with his.

"I want you to sleep in my bed," she said softly. "I need you, Cole."

I need you. Not, I need *this*. This time it was, *I need you*. His pulse hammered. He needed her, too. But…

"Bryn, you're hurt."

"I'm not that hurt."

Still his chest felt tight, painful. "I have so many things to regret in my life already, and when I leave Azalea Bend, I don't want there to be more. I don't want you to have any regrets, either."

He couldn't bear to see regret in her eyes. Not again. And he didn't know where all of this was going—the investigation into Aimee's murder, or his feelings for Bryn. She was scared now, but when this was over, she'd remember that it was Cole who'd brought all this grief back to her.

"The only thing I'll regret about tonight is if I don't spend it with you."

Her eyes shone with raw need and everything inside him responded, and suddenly it didn't matter how she might feel later. What mattered was how she felt now. She needed him.

His legs were shaking as she took his hand and led the way upstairs. He shut the door of her lamplit room behind them and when he turned back, she'd pulled apart her robe. Beneath, she wore only lace panties.

The robe fell in a soft spill at her feet, then she stripped away that last lacy barrier.

He stood there stunned, taking in the curve of her breasts, the narrow waist, the long legs. She stepped out of the piled material and came directly toward him, slid her hand around the back of his neck, and kissed the last shred of his sanity away. His heart nearly leaped out of his chest when she gently pushed him down so that he fell backward onto the bed, tangling with her. He twisted so that he was half on top of her, feeling all the soft, silky heat of her.

"I don't want to hurt you," he said huskily, but even as he spoke he couldn't resist the feel of her flushed skin under his hands. The mist of desire slid through him and he wanted nothing more than to sink into that mist. Sink into her.

"You're not going to hurt me," she whispered against his mouth. But he forced himself to take it slowly. He wanted to be careful with her, so careful. He shifted so that he lay beside her then he got off the bed.

"Cole—"

"Wait." He forced himself to do at least one thing

right. He left the room, went down the hall, rummaged through the drawer for the purchase he'd made in foolish hope he'd barely let himself believe would be fulfilled. He came back with the protection that they should have had the first time.

She reached for his jeans and tugged them off his hips. It was awkward and sweet and incredibly arousing, this passionate hunger of hers that couldn't wait. Then she straddled him, the rigid peaks of her bare breasts brushing his chest. He reached between them and she was hot and wet, ready and blinding; intense heat filled him. Leaning up into the pale globes of her breasts, he took one hard nipple into his mouth, raking it gently with his teeth as his fingers continued their tender torment inside her. She quivered over him, and he felt the hot surge of her release, but he didn't stop. Couldn't stop. Not now. Not ever.

"Please, Cole, now please." And she fumbled for his erection, sheathing him inside her.

He wanted this to be slow. He wanted to please her and take her so gently, but she rocked over him, and all he could do was focus on the gut-wrenching sweetness of her need, and how much he needed her in return. She cried out as he plunged higher inside her, holding tightly to him, her breaths as raspy sharp as his own. Then she let out a helpless moan and covered his mouth with hers.

He came hard and fast, and there was no stopping it. They clung together in the desperate aftermath for uncounted beats before, shockingly, he felt himself grow hard inside her and he pushed her over onto her back.

"I can't get enough of you, Bryn," he told her.

Her kiss was her response. She pulled him over her and he thrust into her again, felt her tightening around him. Carefully, he rested his weight on his hands on either side of her so as not to crush her. This time, it was softer, gentler but no less soul-consuming.

He left the earth in a splintering of sensation and emotion to the sound of her crying out his name. Then he wrapped her in his arms and held her close.

And nothing, but nothing, was going to hurt her tonight.

If she could have, Bryn would never have left her bed. She woke to Cole's arm draped over her heavy, sated body, holding her curled up against him. She lay there in dreamy half awareness remembering the explosive need and reckless passion of their night together, and she didn't regret one single second they'd shared.

She wondered what it would be like to wake every morning in Cole's arms, and knew how quickly she could grow accustomed to it. A wash of sadness had her opening her eyes, staring at his dark-lashed closed eyes.

I have so many things to regret in my life already, and when I leave Azalea Bend, I don't want there to be more.

His life was in Baton Rouge and hers was tied to Bellefleur, hundreds of years of Louvel history, and her mother. Azalea Bend was a town of ruin to him and there was no way she could be selfish enough to expect him to make it his home. And even if she was willing to leave Bellefleur and go with him, would she forever remind him of everything that had happened fifteen years ago, bringing him more pain than joy? She and Cole had a track record of always destroying each other, and she didn't know how that could change.

She squeezed her eyes shut against a sudden burn of tears and took a deep, steadying breath, choking back the emotion in her throat. One day at a time was all she could handle. She was walking an emotional tightrope as it was. And there was someone out there who'd like to see Cole, or maybe both of them, dead. How could she even be thinking about the future at all?

"Bryn."

She opened her eyes to find Cole's tender morning gaze searching her face.

"Hey," she whispered shakily.

"Are you all right?" He looked so worried.

"I'm fine." She didn't know how to explain what she was feeling without putting him on the spot. "I'm fine as long as you're here."

"I'm not going anywhere," he promised softly.

"Tell me about your life in Baton Rouge," she said.

His hard lips twisted in a half smile. "You want to hear about my job?"

"No. Your life." She wanted to know where he lived, who he saw, what he did.

"I bought an old steamboat gothic house downtown and I fix it up when I'm not working. I go to the museum every once in a while. I run in the park. I work. A lot." He watched her with his serious, impenetrable eyes. "Why?"

"You have girlfriends?"

He smiled again. "Are you going to be jealous if I say yes?"

Her stomach clenched but she tipped her chin at him. "Of course not," she said loftily, but she noticed he hadn't answered her question.

He laughed and pulled himself up. It should have been criminal for a man to look so sexy first thing in the morning, but there he was, all naked and wonderful in her bed. And all she could do was stare at his bare, powerful shoulders, sliding her gaze down to his flat, muscular stomach, and lower… A tight heat hit her and she lifted her eyes to find his hungry, hot look pinning her, telling her he knew just what she was thinking. He had bed head, and it made him so deliciously, dangerously, sexily vulnerable. Then there was nothing vulnerable about him because he was kissing her and touching her in all the warm, heavy places he'd touched her last night, setting her body on fire all over again. He focused his gaze on hers as he entered her in tortuous increments.

She reached up, cradled her hands around his neck,

and held on to him for dear life as he began to thrust into her. She arched to meet him and he responded to the eager motion of her hips with a slow, scorching kiss that stole her breath and her senses. And he rocked her into that perfect, searing sweetness that somehow, this time, wasn't enough to fill the empty, aching spaces inside her.

Cole hated the petrified light that flashed in Bryn's eyes as he checked the rental car thoroughly before they headed out an hour later. She still held herself with a slight stiffness, a hold-over from the bruising accident, and that made his heart crack a little every time he looked at her.

They caught Lizzie Cornelius on her way out the door. She lived in a comfortable new neighborhood of small tract homes on the Baton Rouge side of town.

In her denim dress embroidered with daisies, her auburn hair pulled back in a neat style, Bryn's childhood friend looked every inch the elementary-school teacher.

"I don't have much time this morning," she said when Bryn planted herself firmly in front of her on the small bricked front stoop of her ranch-style house. "It's good to see you, Bryn."

She gave Cole a more unwelcoming look. She hadn't had much to say when he'd interviewed her over the weekend.

"I don't know what I can tell you about Aimee," Lizzie told Bryn.

"You spent as much time with her that summer as I did," Bryn said. "Maybe more." A flicker of something dark shadowed her eyes. "Was Aimee seeing anyone that summer? Anyone special? A boy?"

"Aimee didn't have a boyfriend," Lizzie said immediately.

"Maybe someone who wasn't a boyfriend," Cole interjected. If Aimee hadn't mentioned anything about a pregnancy to Bryn, maybe her liaison had been secret. But still, someone might have seen her somewhere, sometime, with someone and not realized what they were seeing. A lot of people had seen him on occasion with Bryn and had never known they were dating. They'd kept it that secret. Only Aimee had ever known.

Would Aimee have had a secret romance and not even have told Bryn?

Lizzie shook her head. "I can't think of anyone."

"I wonder if you knew any of these boys." Aimee was a homebody, and if she hadn't met a boy from school, then that left Bellefleur. He dug out the list of yard boys and showed it to Lizzie.

"Hmmmm." Lizzie stared at the list. "Actually, she did tell me once that she had a crush on Tommy Navin. But they never dated." She dragged her keys out of her purse. "I've got twenty third-graders waiting for me." Lizzie gave Bryn a quick hug.

Bryn and Cole sat down in the car and watched Lizzie Cornelius drive away down the neat, tidy neighborhood street.

Cole stuck the key in the ignition. "Emile Brouch-ard said Tommy Navin was trouble."

Bryn flashed him a determined look. "I never even heard Aimee mention Tommy Navin's name. I barely remember him. Even Lizzie said they weren't dating."

Edward Navin lived in a white clapboard frame house with flaking paint that exposed chunks of graying wood. A beat-up Ford pickup in the carport suggested he was home.

Which didn't do them much more good than the first time Cole had knocked on his door. Navin was tall, skinny, with a thatch of silver-streaked black hair that looked as if it hadn't been washed lately.

"We want to talk to you about your son," Cole said.

"I already told you I'm not talking about Tommy," the man growled.

"We just want to ask Tommy a few questions," Bryn said. "Can you tell us where he is?"

Navin's narrow face tightened. "I know what you're after. I heard about him in town." He jabbed a finger at Cole. "Been asking questions about that girl who got killed."

"Is Tommy still in Azalea Bend?" Cole asked. He tried to keep his voice polite, but something about the man was getting under his skin.

His flat icy eyes turned mean. "Keep asking questions about Tommy and you'll regret it."

The chipped wooden door slammed in their faces.

Their meeting at the police station wasn't till mid-afternoon. Cole used his cell phone to contact Ken Bryant and ask him to work on the Tommy Navin angle. He wanted to know ASAP if Tommy Navin was in Azalea Bend. They grabbed a quick lunch between repeat visits to old friends of Bryn's and Aimee's. Most of them weren't much more forthcoming than they'd been in their first interview with Cole, though they were a hell of a lot friendlier. So were the yard boys.

Griff Bonner ran a transmission shop out of a huge shed behind his house outside town. A sign out front advertised swamp tours on the side. In the liquid heat, he wiped sweat off his chiseled features with a greasy towel and gave Bryn an appraising look as he came out of the shadows of the garage shop.

He gave Bryn a cocky smile. "Miss Bryn Louvel," he said. "I've been just waiting for the day you'd come see me." He didn't bother with Cole.

"You remember the summer you worked at Bellefleur?" she asked.

Bonner shrugged. "Sure. He already asked me about it." He jerked his head at Cole, but he didn't take his eyes off Bryn. "I don't know who killed her. Always thought it was that Dempsey guy. My dad saw him in the bar that night. He said he was nuts."

"What I was really wondering was whether you knew if she was involved with anyone," Bryn said coolly. "Did you ever see her around Bellefleur with anybody?"

"You mean like a boyfriend?"

"Like that," Cole said tightly. "Like Tommy Navin, maybe."

Bryn shot him a glance.

"Sure," Bonner said. "She hung out with Tommy."

Bryn blinked and her head swiveled back to Bonner. "She did?"

"Yeah. He used to brag about doing her."

Chapter 15

Harlan Michel's office was dominated by faded black-and-white photographs of spillway construction, lumber trains cutting through swamps and oil rigs heading downriver for the Gulf. The St. Salome Parish police chief kept them waiting twenty minutes in the outer office before he sauntered out to usher them in.

Chief Michel creaked into the chair behind his nicked metal-framed desk, gesturing Cole and Bryn toward a pair of tattered orange seats pulled up on the other side. The chief's massive size dwarfed the small room. The fluorescent light overhead gave a sheeny glare to his bald head.

Bryn hadn't said anything on the drive over from Griff Bonner's. Cole had let her be. Truth was, he didn't know what to say, how to break through that brittle shell of guilt she was building around herself in regard to Aimee's death.

She got right down to business. "I want the investigation into my sister's murder reopened."

Harlan Michel leaned back and propped his broad hands on his equally broad stomach. "Now, Miss Louvel, that case was closed a mighty long time ago. I already told Mr. Dempsey here that we aren't going to be reopening it."

"Fifteen years," Bryn cut in. "But Wade Dempsey didn't kill Aimee."

"You remember this." Cole handed a copy of the forensic report to the chief. He leaned forward, took it in his thick fingers and examined it.

"Yes, I do, you already showed me this. It doesn't mean much if Randol Ormond is in such bad health he can't testify." Michel eyed Cole with his heavy gaze. "Where is the original, by the way?"

"I'm in the process of retaining an expert to examine the original, then it will be turned over to your office," Cole explained. "An expert can testify that it wasn't tampered with. As I told you, I spoke to Randol Ormond in Florida at a rest home and he gave this document to me. I believe the forensic report was suppressed on the order of Hugh Cavanaugh, and replaced with a version that removed any mention of the scrapings from beneath Aimee's nails that would have cleared my father."

"And I told you that wasn't enough to reopen the case," Michel said.

"I'm now prepared to have Aimee's body exhumed," Bryn added, her voice steady, too steady, masking the anguish the taut set of her mouth revealed. "New tests will prove that she didn't struggle with Wade Dempsey that night and can be used to connect the real killer to the crime."

"Maybe." The chief's expression was noncommittal. "We don't have a budget for dredging up old crimes—"

"This isn't an old crime," Bryn said, heat entering her voice. "I'm sure you know someone cut the brake lines on Cole's car a couple of nights ago. He's been asking questions around town about Aimee. Someone doesn't like that, and whoever that is might be the person who killed Aimee."

The chief was shaking his head, but Bryn didn't give him time to speak.

"Aimee might have been pregnant when she died," she said in a low, husky voice that Cole knew meant she was on the verge of tears. "And she might have been seeing Tommy Navin. Do you know if Tommy Navin still lives in St. Salome Parish?"

Harlan Michel frowned. "I don't know about that," he said. "Look, Miss Louvel, this still isn't much to go on."

Bryn lifted her chin, and Cole could see her drawing the battle lines, fighting back the emotion that brimmed so near the surface. "There's a murderer walking the streets in Azalea Bend, Chief Harlan. Cole's brake lines—"

"You don't know that's connected," the Chief interrupted.

"You don't know it's not," Bryn said. Her voice shook and she took a breath to even it. "Surely the possibility that there's a murderer stalking free in this town is important enough for you to squeeze at least one officer out of your budget to assign to this case. And just so you know, I've been in touch with an investigative reporter at a cable network who's interested in showcasing Aimee's murder on an upcoming program. Frank Skelly was the police chief who bungled this case fifteen years ago. You have a chance to be the one who makes sure it's not bungled this time."

Well, she had a couple of calls in to some cable networks, so it wasn't a complete lie even if they hadn't called back. The challenge in her eyes was enough to hold the chief silent for a tense beat.

"The Louvel name still means something in this town, Chief Harlan." She tossed in her final card. "And it means something in this state. This story is going to get coverage. Big coverage. You don't want it to reflect badly on you when it does."

"Now, Miss Louvel, I didn't say we weren't going

to follow up on this information," he said in a much more agreeable drawl. "I suppose I could assign one of my officers to look into the case."

Cole placed his hand over Bryn's. Her fingers gripping the metal edge of the orange chair were shaking. She looked at him, and he gave her a grim smile as he squeezed her cold fingers before he turned back to the chief.

"We'd like a detective assigned today," Cole said firmly. "Unless you can explain to reporters that you've got another murder under investigation in Azalea Bend right now that's taking up your time." He cocked a dubious brow as he continued to level his hard gaze. "There has already been an attempt on my life that could have cost Bryn hers. This is not the time for delay unless you want another body on your hands."

The chief's mouth set in an annoyed line. "I'll have an officer get in touch with you today."

"Thank you." He gave the chief his cell number and asked him to have the officer who was assigned the job contact him as soon as possible. "I've been working with a private investigator, and Bryn and I have already been interviewing people who knew Aimee that summer. We'd be happy to share what we've found out so far with the officer."

They'd managed to skirt the issue of Randol Ormond's MIA status, to Cole's relief. In the meantime, maybe they'd find him.

Heat smothered them as they left the law-enforce-
ment building and crossed the street to the parked
rental car. He could see the paranoia in Bryn's darkened gaze. She glanced around as if she half expected
a car to appear and try to run them down.

"You did great in there," Cole said, taking her hand
as they crossed to the car. He opened the door for
Bryn, wishing he could find some way to take that
scared look out of her eyes. "You did it. You fought
for Aimee."

Bryn's expression didn't relax. "They don't want
to reopen it. If something happens to us, they'll shut
it down that quick. And we don't really have a cable
network covering the crime, remember?" She sat
down in the passenger seat and Cole went around to
the other side.

He keyed the ignition, his insides twisting. She
was good and stressed all over again. "Let's go back
to Bellefleur." He reached over and took her chin in
his hands, pulling her agonized, lovely gaze to him.
"You've had enough of this today."

The plantation waited in the cloudy murk of the afternoon. More rain threatened, and the dark gloom of
the house against the forbidding sky made him wish
he could turn right around and leave it. Take Bryn
away, somewhere airy and bright and safe.

She keyed the lock in the front door and pushed it
open. Cole shut it behind them, closing out the buzz
of the tractor where Emile Brouchard continued to dig

up one of the wild side gardens. Bryn went straight to her office.

"I have to call Drake," she said quietly. "He deserves to know what we're doing. He's part of this, too."

Cavanaugh wasn't going to like what they'd done. Cole watched Bryn punch in the numbers on the phone, her face cast in tired lines. He wanted to do nothing more than gather her into his arms and hold her, but she'd been withdrawing from him all day. He didn't know what to do to pierce her shield. And maybe she was right to keep her heart shielded. If he was smart, he'd do the same.

But he wasn't very smart around Bryn.

"Drake?"

Cole watched Bryn lean her forehead into one hand while she held the phone and told Cavanaugh about the accident, the calls to the cable networks, the request to reopen the case.

"We're in the process of retaining an expert to examine the forensic document." She was quiet another long beat, listening to Cavanaugh. "People aren't going to blame you for what your father might have done," Bryn insisted softly. "It's not your fault. And I can't walk away from it. I have to find out what happened to Aimee. There's a murderer out there." She rubbed her forehead. "Have you had a chance yet to go through your father's things? Have you found anything?"

She lifted her head, squeezed her eyes shut for a minute, then put the phone down and looked at Cole.

"He hung up. He's pretty upset." Emotion gleamed in her eyes. "And he's right. It's not fair, but this could damage his campaign. Look at what happened to me. It's not my fault, but Mrs. Guidry cancelled events at Bellefleur. Drake could lose his campaign over this if it goes public about Hugh Cavanaugh sabotaging a murder investigation to protect my father. Hugh Cavanaugh's still a well-known name, not just in Azalea Bend. He served in the state congress, too, and he did a stint as transportation commissioner. Drake rose so quickly in politics on his father's name, and this could really hurt him."

She hadn't turned the light on in the office when she'd gone in to make the call, and in the cloudy dark, her eyes looked impossibly exhausted.

"He's coming in to Azalea Bend tomorrow. He's going to talk to Chief Michel. I know he's going to try to get this stopped."

"It's too late for that, Bryn."

"I feel awful," she said shakily. "I don't want to hurt him."

"You can't beat yourself up over this, Bryn," he said gently. "We're doing what we have to do."

She nodded, but she didn't look any happier.

"You called Drake a friend," he said suddenly. "But he asked you to marry him." Cavanaugh's relationship with Bryn bothered him, and he didn't know if it was more than jealousy or not. He didn't like this new, possessive part of himself that had come out since he'd returned to Azalea Bend.

"We were always friends," Bryn told him. "But after Aimee died, we got closer. It wasn't romantic. Or at least, not on my part. Then, somehow, it changed. And I didn't realize it had changed. I should have known, should have said something. He would come into town every once in a while and we'd meet for dinner. A few weeks ago, he told me he wanted more. He wanted to get married. I was shocked, and I told him I'd think about it. But then—"

"Then what?" He waited, tension he couldn't define scraping his veins.

"I told him last week that I couldn't marry him. I thought he was all right with it, but I'm not sure he is. And now, all of this is happening. I feel as if I've lost a friend."

She looked so sad, and he didn't know what to say. The truth was, if she was through with Cavanaugh, he'd be glad. He'd never liked Drake and he didn't like him now.

The phone chirped beside her. Bryn looked at it tiredly as if she couldn't stand to talk to one more person, and Cole reached over and picked it up.

"Bellefleur."

"This is Detective Joe Wardell, Azalea Bend Police. I'm looking for Cole Dempsey or Bryn Louvel. I've been assigned the Aimee Louvel case."

Well. Chief Harlan Michel hadn't wasted any time.

Whatever mess had been made fifteen years ago, Michel didn't want to be tainted with it. Cole gave Bryn a thumbs-up as he sat down in the chair opposite her desk. "It's the officer assigned to the case," he told her, cupping his palm over the phone. "This is Cole Dempsey," he told the detective.

Bryn waited, eyes awake now.

"I'd like to set up a time I can meet with you and Miss Louvel tomorrow," Wardell said. "I'd like to come to Bellefleur since the murder occurred there, see the scene for myself. What time would you be available?"

Cole looked at Bryn. "Any time tomorrow would be fine." Bryn nodded.

Wardell suggested one o'clock. "I'd like to go ahead and get some information from you now," he went on. "The chief passed the forensic document on to me that you left with him. And he also mentioned you had been interviewing some of the people here in town."

Cole gave him a rundown of the information he'd given the chief.

"I've got a few hours before I go off duty tonight," the detective told him when he finished. "I'm going to do my best to find out if Tommy Navin is still in Azalea Bend. I'll see you at one tomorrow."

The detective gave Cole his cell number then hung up. Bryn watched Cole with anxious eyes.

He reached across for her hand. It felt small and cold in his. "We're not in this alone anymore, Bryn."

* * *

They fixed dinner together. It was eerily domestic. Bryn would never have thought to imagine Cole working in a kitchen, but he seemed at ease as he whipped together a simple sauce for the fresh shrimp Bryn had picked up over the weekend. She peeled the shrimp while he seemed to enjoy himself digging through her herbs and spices, selecting the ingredients to season the dish. She finally contented herself sitting back and watching, enjoying the lean-shouldered look of him in his dark T-shirt and snug jeans. She could look at him forever, and that was scary.

She liked him in her kitchen far too much.

"I didn't know you cooked," she said after they sat down to the meal.

"I have a lot of talents you don't know about," Cole said.

He gave her a hot look across the table that sent remembered sweetness curling low inside her. She wanted to tell him that she wished she knew more about those talents. She wished they were having a normal relationship that wasn't strung tight by murder and grief and regret.

"Is it all right for you to be gone all this time?" She wondered how long it would be before he had to leave Azalea Bend. And her.

He nodded. "I took a leave from the firm. They understood what I had to do, and why. They know about my father."

"That's why you became a lawyer, isn't it?" she asked quietly. "Your father. Or did you always want to be a lawyer?" She didn't remember him ever mentioning an ambition to go to law school, but then she hadn't known he'd lived off the swamps either. She hadn't really known him fifteen years ago. And she wasn't completely sure she knew him now.

"I don't think the idea crystallized in my mind until several years later," he said. "But yes, it was because of my father. Even if he'd lived, he might not have had a chance in Azalea Bend. Too often, defendants like my father—who can't afford to pay for representation—are left to the mercy of attorneys who don't believe in them and don't much care."

"You care," she said softly, watching him, a sense of pride creeping into her heart.

He rested his fork on the side of his plate, then pushed it back. "I give a lot of money and time to a free legal aid clinic in the city. The money I make from Granville, Piers and Rousseau makes that possible. That Cobra wasn't even bought by me," he told her. "The firm gives them to all the attorneys when they make partner."

He was so much more than she'd realized—fifteen years ago and now. And he'd managed to turn his grief into something positive.

"I'm impressed," she said.

"Don't be." Cole's gaze turned grim. "What I do is for myself as much as anyone else. I swore the day

I left Azalea Bend that I would never feel that way again. Hopeless. Defeated. Powerless. My father was a nothing and a nobody to the police and the prosecution in St. Salome Parish. But to me and my mother, he was our whole life. And they just threw him away."

Her family had held all the power back then. Her family had made him feel powerless. And her family still held power in this town. It was her family name they'd used to get the chief's attention.

Even now, all of Cole's money wasn't as powerful as the Louvel name.

Drake's words whispered in her mind. *He's playing you, Bryn.*

His lean-shouldered, tall frame wasn't that of the boy who'd made that painful vow to himself, but the hurt and hunger in his eyes was the haunting remnant. Now, more than ever, she understood that everything in his life was driven by what had happened fifteen years ago.

And fiercely, she knew she wanted more from him, from this relationship. She couldn't, wouldn't let herself believe Drake was right, that Cole was playing her, but when it came down to it, was Aimee's murder the only thing between them?

The thought of it broke her heart.

Something loud hit the front of the house.

It took a confused second for Bryn to realize it was the front door. Someone was pounding on the front door.

Cole was ahead of her, already out of the kitchen. He flipped on the chandelier in the front hall.

The thunderous blows on the door hadn't stopped. Cole jerked it wide. Bryn stood in the opening from the hallway to the kitchen.

Edward Navin's bloodshot eyes fired at them from the shadows of the portico.

Chapter 16

Cole barely registered his intention before Edward Navin struck out. He rocked sideways, lessening the impact, but the blow still connected. Instant pain roared, but instinct and adrenaline took over. The strong odor of alcohol wafted around him as something shattered against the hall floor.

Cole followed with a jab that sent the older man stumbling backward. Navin hit the doorjamb, blood spurting from his mouth and nose.

"Call the police, Bryn," Cole hissed. Dammit, he'd opened the door on this drunk and Bryn had nearly paid for it. "Get out of here," he ordered Navin, but Navin wasn't finished and he was blocking the door.

Navin straightened, reeling slightly. "Stop asking questions about Tommy," he slurred. "Tommy didn't kill Aimee Louvel."

"The police are on their way." Bryn appeared in the doorway of the office. She looked pale, shivery. Glass and liquid shimmered over the entry floor. The smell of whiskey hit him again. That's what Navin had struck him with—the bottle of whiskey.

"Bitch! Leave Tommy alone! Both of you!" Blood spat from Navin's mouth. He took a threatening step and Cole stepped in front of him.

"What don't you want the police to find out about Tommy?" Cole demanded, blocking his path to Bryn. "Did Tommy have sex with Aimee Louvel? Did he get Aimee pregnant? Where was Tommy the night Aimee Louvel died?"

"He was at home!" Navin hissed drunkenly. "He didn't have anything to do with it! And if you don't stop asking questions about him, I'll kill you myself. You and that stupid Louvel bitch. Just shut up about my son. He's none of your goddamn business." He coughed and spat out something sharp and white. "You broke my tooth, you bastard," he mumbled crazily.

"You came here looking for trouble and you got it," Cole grated harshly. Adrenaline was wearing off and his head throbbed like hell. "Where is Tommy? Is he in Azalea Bend?"

But Navin was done talking. He took a stumbling lunge forward, fist flying. Cole blocked him with his arm, but the damn drunk wouldn't stop coming. He threw a punch that connected with Navin's jaw and the man reeled backward again, this time onto the portico. He hit the portico floor with a thud, his head lolling back. Blood and spittle oozed from his mouth. He didn't move.

Cole looked at Bryn. She stared back, her eyes huge and anguished.

"Are you all right?" she whispered.

"I'm fine," he told her. She wasn't hurt, that was all that counted. "I think he's out." He looked back at Navin, needing to be sure. He didn't take his eyes off the man.

They waited in the damp heat of the threatening night. Lights rayed through the oaks, and a police cruiser came to a stop beside Edward Navin's beat-up Ford.

Officer Martin Bouvier strode up the steps.

"He came here making threats," Cole told him. "He was drunk, angry about the questions we were asking about Tommy."

"I heard the chief reopened the investigation into your sister's death." Martin looked at Bryn. "You think Tommy had something to do with it?"

"Maybe," Bryn said quietly. "We don't even know if Tommy's still in Azalea Bend."

"I couldn't get anything out of him," Cole said.

"He's a drunk. I've picked him up more times than I can count. He's a mean drunk, too. You got off easy." He finished taking their statement, poked his notebook back in his pocket. "I could use some help getting him to the car."

Cole helped Bouvier muscle Edward Navin's heavy, limp body into the back of the cruiser.

"We'll get his car out of here in the morning," the officer said. "Lock up."

Cole turned back to Bryn in the empty silence after the cruiser disappeared through the black shadows of the oaks.

"You're not okay," she said softly.

"Trust me, I'm okay." Cole went to her and did what he'd wanted to do for the last half hour. He enfolded her cold, soft body in his arms, inhaled her fresh, sweet jessamine scent. She was trembling, and he realized with a shock that he was, too.

He would have fought to the death for her. But all he could do was hold her, tightly, and the fierceness of her embrace in return left his heart in aching pain.

She drew in a shaky breath finally and pulled back. She looked around the glass-strewn hall. "I'm tired of cleaning up floors," she said.

"I hope this will be over soon," Cole said, though he had no way of promising her that. "They'll question Navin in the morning. They'll find out where Tommy is."

"I can't believe he killed Aimee." Her eyes glistened damply. "I can't believe she was pregnant. I can't believe she was having an affair with Tommy Navin and never told me."

"We don't know that yet," Cole told her gently. "But we're going to find out. Whatever happened, we're going to find out. And we'll deal with it together."

Bryn's eyes were still brimming with tears, but she valiantly blinked them back, refused to allow them to escape.

She touched his face. "You're hurt. Let me do something. Get a cold towel, some ice."

He didn't think that would help, but he could see she needed to do something. He locked up the house, went around to every door and window while she got an ice pack from the kitchen. They cleaned up the foyer floor together. Upstairs, she laid the cold pack on his jaw and curled up beside him. He touched her hair, her back, the silky curve of her shoulder, reassuring himself that she was fine, that she was safe.

In the long inky haunt of night, he lay awake. The house creaked and moaned its age in the growing wind of the portending storm.

The ringing phone woke them.

Bryn twisted to reach it, the sheet and Cole's protecting arm falling away, sweeping morning chill across her skin. He watched her with his sexy, slumberous eyes as she answered the phone.

"Bryn? This is Dana."

She blinked for a second, trying to wake up her brain and almost said Dana who? before she remembered. She hadn't talked to many childhood friends since graduation.

"Dana. Hi." She looked back at Cole. His sleepy gaze focused.

"I just got back into town and I had a message from Cole Dempsey." Dana Kellman was silent for a beat. "He wanted me to call him back. He wanted to talk about Aimee. I wanted to call you first."

"We've gotten the investigation into Aimee's death reopened," Bryn explained. "So he's probably not the last person who'll be calling you. I'm sorry."

"Why is the case being reopened?"

Bryn explained briefly about the forensic report and Randol Ormond. Then she told Dana about the accident. Dana gasped.

"Oh, my God, Bryn. I'm glad you're all right."

"I'm fine, Dana. Really. I just wanted you to know how important this is—if there's anything you know about what Aimee was doing that summer, we need to know."

"I'll help you if I can," Dana said. "But I don't know how I could."

"Did you ever think there was anyone else who might have had a reason to kill her?" Bryn asked.

"No," Dana said immediately. "I mean, you know how sweet she was."

"I know." Bryn swallowed thickly. "What about a boyfriend? Do you know if she was seeing anyone that summer?"

"She didn't have a boyfriend as far as I know."

"What about Tommy Navin?" Bryn probed softly.

"What about him?" Dana sounded confused.

"Was Aimee seeing Tommy Navin? Lizzie told me Aimee said she had a crush on him that summer. And Tommy's father acted pretty strangely when we tried to talk to him about Tommy. He wouldn't tell us where he is now, didn't even like us asking questions about Tommy. And last night he came over here and made some threats."

Dana was silent.

"Dana, if there's anything you aren't telling me, I need you to tell me now. Erica Saville said the day Aimee died, she went to Boudreaux's with Aimee. She said Aimee was asking questions that made her think Aimee was pregnant. If she was pregnant with Tommy Navin's baby—"

"Aimee? Pregnant?" Dana made a disbelieving sound. "No way. And not with Tommy Navin's baby, I can tell you that for sure."

"What do you mean?"

"Tommy Navin is gay."

Bryn's heart stumbled. "What?"

"I ran into Tommy about five years ago, in a club in New Orleans. Some girlfriends and I went down to the Quarter. We were just being crazy and we went into this place called Coco Creole. Tommy was working there. I didn't even recognize him at first, but he knew me. I swear, he was dressed in this sparkly sheath dress and a Marilyn Monroe wig. He was wearing makeup and a boa and high heels. He had this cross-dressing act. He sang—he was actually really good—and afterward, he came over and talked to me."

Bryn stared at Cole. "What did he say?"

Cole sat up, leaned close to Bryn to listen in with her.

"I told him I was living in New Orleans now," Dana explained, "and he talked about how glad he was to get out of Azalea Bend and away from his dad. You know, he was always kind of weird in high school and in trouble a lot. He got in fights all the time, and he told me how screwed up he was. He was always trying to prove he was a man. His dad suspected he was gay, and he beat him up all the time at home. Anyway, I can tell you he didn't have anything to do with Aimee's murder. He really cared about Aimee."

"What do you mean?"

"Aimee helped him. She talked to him a lot that summer, and he confided in her that he was gay. She felt sorry for him—she knew about his dad and everything. She told me and Lizzie Cornelius that she had a crush on him. I thought it was just weird at the time, but now I know why. She was trying to take the heat off Tommy by talking about having a crush on him, and Tommy said she'd told him he could tell people they were involved."

He always talked about doing her. Bryn wondered if those had really been Tommy's words or if Griff

Bonner had elaborated, but either way, now at least it made some sense. Aimee had always looked out for those who needed help—even at her own expense. But at the same time, her head reeled. What did this mean? If Aimee hadn't been involved with Tommy, if Aimee hadn't been pregnant, then why had she been asking Erica Saville those questions?

"I never knew," Bryn whispered, her chest tight. "Aimee never said anything to me about Tommy."

"She wouldn't have told you," Dana said. "She promised Tommy she wouldn't tell anyone. And she probably didn't try to give you the line about having a crush on him because you would have known she was lying. Even Lizzie and I thought it was strange. But you would have known."

Bryn swallowed thickly. Would she? More than ever, she felt as if she'd let Aimee down. She'd been so self-absorbed that summer.

She felt Cole's arm slide around her, his strong touch giving comfort.

"That was just like Aimee, you know," Dana said. "She'd do stuff for people. And if Tommy's dad was over there making threats, it's because he never wanted anyone to know Tommy was gay and he's probably still afraid it's going to come out. He didn't even come to Tommy's funeral."

"What?" Bryn gasped. She still hadn't had time to process everything Dana had already told her. "Tommy's dead?"

"He was killed in a car accident a couple of years ago. I stayed in touch with him after we ran into him at the Coco Creole and some of his friends contacted me when he died."

They couldn't even talk to Tommy now. And Tommy hadn't been in Azalea Bend this past week. Tommy hadn't gotten Aimee pregnant or really even been involved with her.

Bryn put down the phone a few minutes later after saying goodbye to Dana. She looked at Cole's grim face.

They'd thought they had a lead. They'd thought they might be close. But they were farther away from the truth than ever. The pieces still weren't fitting, and her head hurt from trying to put them all together. The more she found out about Aimee's last summer, the less the pieces made sense.

And for the first time she wondered what would happen if they never did.

The weight of the graying day pressed down on Bellefleur. The brewing storm that had been menacing the skies since yesterday had yet to break open. Meanwhile, the clouds built and the pressure tightened.

Even the marsh grasses weren't whispering today.

Cole's stomach felt like one big ball of stress that would never come loose. He'd troubleshot Bryn's car after Detective Wardell had left, and figured out all she needed was a new battery. They'd gone into town for it—she'd insisted on paying for her new battery as if it was some badge of honor to pay for it herself when she was clearly flat broke.

She hadn't had much to say since the detective had left, and their trip into town had been tense. Wardell had been a burly bear of man who'd been sympathetic but not encouraging. Edward Navin had confessed to nailing the chicken bone to Bryn's door, but he'd denied having anything to do with Cole's brake lines being cut or the brick. It was clear Wardell wasn't convinced, and they were still holding Navin.

The only good news was that Frank Skelly, the chief of police at the time of Aimee's murder, had agreed to meet with Chief Michel. Apparently Skelly wanted to see the forensic document for himself.

And according to Wardell, Skelly was bringing an attorney with him.

Cole's own investigator had confirmed the information about Tommy, at least in terms of the bare facts. He'd worked at the Coco Creole and been killed in a traffic accident two years ago.

"I want you to come to Baton Rouge with me," Cole told Bryn. They were standing in the kitchen at Bellefleur. She was chopping sandwich fixings as if she was about to feed an army. Her nerves were like elastic stretched way too far and he didn't want to see her break. "At least for a few nights. You need to get away from all of this."

She looked at him, her face pale in the eerie storm-light that crept through the kitchen window. Outside, he could see Emile Brouchard rounding a shed, and further, the glow from Patsy Louvel's cottage windows. Wind started to whip a fierce dance through the trees, and Mr. Brouchard put his head down against the blustering air.

"I can't do that," she said. "My mother is here."

"We'll take her with us."

"Maybe I should rephrase that. I don't *want* to do that. I don't want just to run away."

"I put you in this position, Bryn," he said grimly. The heavy weight of that fact shuddered deep inside him. "I'm not leaving you alone here. Especially not now. The more the authorities ask questions, the more dangerous this could become. I have a responsibility to keep you safe. Whoever is out there has already proven they don't like the questions we're asking."

"I'm not your responsibility," she responded heatedly. She put the knife down and looked at him. "And I might not even be in danger. Maybe Edward Navin *did* cut your brake lines. He's a crazy drunk. He's capable of anything."

There was a flicker of something sharp in her eyes, and he saw, just for that instant, what she was trying to hide from him. She was scared, but so was he.

"As long as you're in danger, I'm not leaving, Bryn. We're stirring something up here. We just don't know what yet. Skelly's not bringing an attorney to Azalea Bend with him because he's innocent."

"Maybe he's just being cautious," Bryn said. "They're still holding Navin. He could be behind everything that's happened. Either way, you can't stay here forever. You can't be my keeper. I've lived by myself at Bellefleur for years, you know."

"Do you think finding the truth about Aimee is the only reason I'm still here?" Cole asked roughly.

She didn't answer for a long beat.

"You needed me—you needed me to give you names, information," she said finally. "You needed my help to get Aimee's body exhumed, the Louvel name to get people to open their doors and answer questions, to get the Chief to re-open the case. Would you have come back to Azalea Bend if not for Aimee's murder?"

He didn't know how to convince her that what was happening between them was bigger than what had drawn then together. And the truth was, she was partly right. He'd come here to use her, and he wouldn't deny it though he was ashamed of it at the same time.

He'd thought his heart was dead to her. But it hadn't been, and using her wasn't why he'd stayed. It wasn't enough for him to believe it, though. She had to believe it, too.

"It doesn't matter why I came back," he said.

"It matters to me." She lifted cold, tormented eyes to him.

She was pushing him away. He knew it, yet it yanked at old bitterness inside him.

"We can't get this—thing—between us confused with anything real," she went on in a small voice. "We're in a situation filled with high emotion and stress. And when it's over, you're going to go back to Baton Rouge."

The stress in his stomach balled tighter. He wanted to tell her that he wanted her to come to Baton Rouge with him, more than for a few nights, but how far out on this limb could he go alone? "I'm not confused, Bryn." Pride lodged anything more in his throat.

She stared at him in the pale gloam streaming through the window, and he saw what he'd known all along. She hadn't given him her complete trust fifteen years ago, and she wasn't ready to give it to him now. They'd always been from different worlds. And although his world now was on par with hers, she'd have to step off that track laid down from birth to see it.

And there wasn't a damn thing he could do about it.

The phone shrilled through the premature night from the direction of the office. Bryn raced through the house, and he followed her. Her face was drawn, tense, as she held the phone.

"We're both here," she said. "Come now."

She put it down and he waited.

"That was Drake," she said. "He's at his house in town. He'll be here in a few minutes. He's found something in his father's papers he says we need to see."

Chapter 17

The waiting was awful. Cole didn't speak, only paced the portico outside. Their conversation in the kitchen clung to the very air between them and she couldn't bear it.

She went back into the office and pretended to go through some bills. She'd left the door open and when she heard Drake's car, she went outside. Lightning cracked the darkening sky and the storm bore down. The chandelier in the foyer snapped.

They'd lost electricity.

"I need a drink," Drake said.

He looked as though he'd already had a few. His face was pale, and he was shaking. He wore a suit, but it looked like he'd slept in it. Bryn tried to take his arm, but he shook her off and Cole strode to her side. His eyes were forbidding and cold.

"Bryn said you told her you found something," Cole said. "What is it?"

Rain began to pour and wind whipped around them. "Let's go inside," she insisted.

They followed Drake into the parlor. He held a thin folder and when he sat down, he kept it clasped firmly in his hand.

The air in the shadowed parlor was thick as she lit an amber oil lamp and several candles. A warm glow filled the darkened room. Cole sat with her on the rosewood Victorian settee across from Drake.

"I went home last night," Drake said. "To my house here in town. I went through my father's things." He looked at Cole for a second, then locked his roiling storm-gray gaze back on Bryn. "I wish you hadn't done this, Bryn. I wish you hadn't let Cole Dempsey come back here and bring all this up. You can't help Aimee. It's too late. It's fifteen years too late."

"I have to know who killed her," Bryn said. The house was warm, humid, but she felt shivery as she watched Drake.

His fingers gripping the folder were white-knuckled in the flickering amber light.

"I had to live with this all these years," Drake said. Bryn leaned forward to hear him. His voice burned low and the storm outside raged. Wind shook the shutters. "I called Harlan Michel today. I can't stop him. Goddammit, Bryn, I can't stop him. He's ordered Aimee's exhumation, said you agreed and Dempsey's got some private medical examiner who's going to oversee the whole thing. Michel's got it in his head he's going to be a big star. He's been in touch with Frank Skelly and Skelly's going to talk."

"Your father and Ormond and Skelly did this to-gether," Cole said harshly. "They covered this up to-gether. How long have you known?"

His eyes were fixed on that folder in Drake's hands.

"I want to make a deal," Drake said. "It doesn't all have to come out, Bryn. The truth isn't just going to hurt me. It's going to hurt you, too."

Bryn's heart stumbled. What was he saying? She didn't want to believe her friend—her *best* friend—had had something to do with Aimee's death, but every word that came out of Drake's mouth was making it all too shockingly real that he knew, had known some-thing, for a very long time. She could barely think.

"Are you saying you know who killed Aimee? Are you saying you've known all this time?" she breathed tightly. "Did you always know?"

Drake's gaze seared her. "I was there for you after Aimee died. I was there for you for fifteen years. Where was Dempsey?"

"Who killed Aimee?" Bryn demanded. She would have gotten out of her seat, taken him by the throat whether that was smart or not, but Cole pressed his hand down on her arm, clamping her in place. "Who killed Aimee?" she repeated.

"The hell of it is, I don't know." Drake's voice cut the harsh tension. "But I know what my bastard of a father thought. He thought I did it."

Bryn felt something sick fill her chest.

"I went to see Aimee that night," Drake continued in a hollow, dead voice. "I called her and she wouldn't talk to me. When I got here, she was outside by the reflecting pond. She said she was waiting for you."

His awful gaze locked on Bryn.

"She was upset, and she wouldn't listen to me. I told her I was in love with her, had been in love with her since, hell, I couldn't remember. I think I was always in love with her. She was different, like an angel. She was softer than you, Bryn. She was sweeter."

Bryn didn't move. She had to know, and didn't want to know at the same time. "What happened then?"

"I poured my heart out to her and she told me I was just a friend."

The sick feeling crawled up Bryn's throat. In all the years since, Drake had been her best friend, and he'd wanted to be more. And she'd told him he was just a friend. But it was Aimee he'd wanted. She'd been a replacement for Aimee.

"She kept talking about Wade Dempsey, and Cole and Bryn, and how she needed to fix something. She told me to leave, that I was going to be in the way. I was angry. I tried to grab her. I just wanted her attention. I just wanted her to listen to me."

"Oh, God," Bryn breathed.

Cole's hand on her arm didn't move.

"What then?" Cole's voice grated low and fierce.

"We struggled. She scratched my face and arms." Drake's gray eyes burned silver fire across the room. "She was alive when I left, I swear it. But my father saw me come in when I got home. I told him I'd been to the Louvels'. Then the call came in about Aimee. He thought I'd killed her. My own father. He thought I'd done it. He got together with Ormond and Skelly and they made sure no one knew I'd been at Bellefleur that night. They got rid of the DNA. They railroaded Wade Dempsey, and for all I knew, Wade Dempsey had done it."

His fiery gaze swung to Cole. "I don't know who killed her, I swear. If it wasn't your father, what the hell does it matter now? It wasn't me, either, but if you go back to Aimee's body for more DNA, they're going to find mine. I was there that night, and Skelly knows it. Skelly will turn on me in a heartbeat to save himself. If that original forensic report is authenticated, we're all going down. Me, Skelly, Ormond. But none of them killed Aimee, and I didn't either."

"We have to find the truth, Drake." Bryn didn't know whether she believed him or not about leaving Aimee alive that night. Her head was reeling.

"You don't want the truth, Bryn. Trust me, you don't want the truth. The truth isn't going to solve anything. It's going to make everything worse. The truth is going to ruin my career. And it's going to ruin your mother's name. It's all going to come out."

Bryn felt the blood drain from her face. "What are you talking about?" She didn't recognize her own voice, it was so reedy and faint.

"I want a deal, Bryn," Drake said.

"What kind of deal?" Cole asked in a forbidding tone.

Drake got to his feet, strode across the room to stand behind a table that held a decanter of brandy and several glasses. He put the folder down on the table and poured a trembling glass of alcohol.

Cole moved his hand from her arm. Bryn watched him pull the cell phone out of his pocket. Her gaze locked with his. His look was grim.

"Get out, Bryn," he said beneath his breath and pushed the cell phone into her hand. "Get help."

Drake shot back the glass of brandy as Bryn stood.

"I want the original forensic report," Drake said. "Without that, everything else falls apart. Especially now that I got rid of Ormond. And for the document, you'll get what's in this folder."

"What happened to Randol Ormond?" Bryn asked.

"I called him. I told him he didn't have a prayer. I told him I was going to kill him with my bare hands if he didn't disappear. I know through some old friends where his daughter lives. I told him I'd kill her and her whole family, too. He thinks I killed Aimee. He believed my threats. I don't know where the hell he went."

"Get out of here, Bryn," Cole said again.

But Drake moved first, streaking his hand inside his jacket pocket. He pointed a gun at Bryn, freezing her in place. Cole took to his feet and Drake swung the gun on him.

"Drop the phone, Bryn," Drake ordered.

She dropped it. It hit the pine floor with a crack and splintered into several pieces. She watched as the battery separated from the cell phone's body, each part flying in a different direction.

"Don't take a step, either one of you." Drake poured another shot without taking his eyes off them. "I don't want to hurt you, Bryn, but I wouldn't mind putting a hole in Dempsey. If I'm going to pay, I'm not going to pay alone."

He lifted the glass, took a sip. The storm beat against the shutters and the oil lamp flickered. He tossed back the rest of the glass and set it down.

"I know you haven't turned the original document over to Harlan Michel," Drake went on in a low, terrifying voice that Bryn barely recognized. "And I've thought through the possibility that you may not have it here. Maybe you have it tucked away in some bank drawer somewhere. If so, that's unfortunate because I'll have to move on to Plan B."

Bryn didn't think she wanted to know what Plan B was. Her friend was holding a gun on her. Her brain felt as though it was on a roller-coaster ride.

"It's upstairs in my briefcase," Cole said suddenly. "I'll go get it."

She swung her head to look at his stern, cold profile. He was controlled, completely controlled. And he was lying.

Drake gave a bitter laugh. "I think we'll get it together, Dempsey."

"I want to know what's in that folder," Cole said.

"The proof that Bryn's slut mother and your low-life father had an affair," Drake said. "And I can promise you, when this story hits, and it's going to hit big, Bryn's mother's name is going to be trashed on every nightly news and cable crime channel in this country. It's nice, tidy hard news that a former state commissioner and prosecutor conspired with a local police chief and coroner to cover up a crime to save his son, but you know it's not going to stop there. Twenty-four-hour cable news runs on the seedier side of every story. And this is a juicy one. Plantation owner shoots the man screwing his wife while his friends in high places cover up the crime. They'll say I killed Aimee. The DNA will fry me and so will Skelly. He wasn't as easy to scare off as Ormond. But they won't forget about your mother, Bryn. I'll make sure of it."

"You're crazy," she breathed. "You should have told the truth then. It would be over now, forgotten.

If you didn't do it, a real investigation would have uncovered the true killer."

"You're right about that," Drake said, and now his voice slurred just a little. His silvery eyes went dark. "My father screwed me. He covered up a murder I didn't commit, trampled the investigation because he didn't believe his own son. And if he thought I looked guilty then, I look a hundred times more guilty now. Even if anyone can eventually prove I didn't do it, what the hell good do you think that's going to do me, Bryn? My political career will be over. Everything I've worked for—gone. I knew about the cover-up from day one. Ormond, Skelly, my father, we're all guilty of obstructing a murder investigation."

He took a step toward them and waved the gun.

"It doesn't have to happen," Drake finished. He picked up the folder from the table. He had the gun in one hand, the folder in the other. Did he really think she'd trade her mother's fifteen-year-old affair for the truth about Aimee's murder? But the crazy light in Drake's eyes told her how desperate he was right now. He was at least half-drunk, too. "None of it has to happen. There's no point. Aimee's dead. Your father's dead. It doesn't matter who killed her. Get me that document and this will all be over."

Cole took Bryn's hand. "Go," he said. He shoved her a little when she didn't move. "Go ahead." He looked at her even as he spoke to Drake. "It's in my room."

God, he wanted her to go upstairs. She locked eyes

with him, and she knew he was lying. That document wasn't upstairs.

They left the flickering spill of the oil lamp. Drake was behind them and she knew he still had that loaded pistol pointed at their backs. Cole pushed her when she hesitated on the stairs. She took a few stumbling steps, then stopped, looked back at him. Drake stood below, the gun gleaming in the storm-light.

"Go up the stairs, Bryn," Cole said quietly.

He wanted her out of the way. She could see it in his haunted, harsh eyes. There was no document upstairs and that could only mean he was going to try something. He was going to get her out of the way, and he was going to tackle Drake.

And he was going to get shot. Because if he didn't, Drake would kill them both.

"Trust me," Cole whispered, and in that surreal beat, she knew that's all he'd asked all along. Ever. It was all he'd asked of her fifteen years ago, and it was all he'd asked of her since he'd come back to Bellefleur. And she'd waited way too late to show him that she did.

And she didn't want to show him this way. She reached for Cole's hand.

"Hurry up," Drake ordered angrily.

Cole pushed Bryn forward. She lost her grip on Cole's hand and fell forward with a jarring thud.

In the spinning pearly-dark, she twisted, saw Cole leap toward Drake. The gun fired through the sound of battering wind.

* * *

Fire slashed through Cole's shoulder. But he might as well have been stung by a bee for all he cared. He hit the foyer floor on top of Drake and the gun skidded sideways.

He grabbed Cavanaugh by the throat and slammed a fist into his jaw that sent the other man's head thudding hard against the wood of the floor. Cole's shoulder screamed and he nearly blacked out, but Cavanaugh wasn't finished. He swung up, connecting fist to chin, knocking Cole sideways.

"Get the gun, Bryn." His voice came out like a scraping, anguished whisper and he was scared to death he was going to lose consciousness. Drake stumbled to his feet and came after him. Cole lunged at him, slamming him forward across the floor. Drake hit the marble table, his head thunking.

Cole wavered on his feet, watching Drake. The other man slumped on the floor, blood spurting from his head.

"I got the gun," Bryn said, her voice wobbling but strong. God, she was so strong. And alive. She was alive. He didn't care what happened now. She handed him the gun and Cole sank down, a misty dark sliding in and out of his vision.

"Call 911," he said.

As if from a distance, he heard Bryn's feet move past him. Then she was back. He worked to clear his vision.

"Dammit! The phones are out!" She ran past him again, to the parlor. She was going for the cell.

He heard her rustling around, followed by several expletives. "The damn phone broke apart and I can't find all of the pieces!" she said desperately. "We have to do something about your wound, Cole. At least until I can get to a working phone."

They had to get help. He had to keep thinking and not lose it. He really didn't want to lose it until he'd told Bryn he loved her.

She'd brought some kind of throw and she tried wrapping it over his shoulder. It might as well have been a doily for all the good it did to stop the blood. She'd brought the oil lamp with her, too. She set it on the rococo table. He struggled to sit back, away from Cavanaugh, where he could at least rest against the base of the steps.

In the lamp's glow, her eyes shone scared as she knelt in front of him, and he wanted to hold her so badly, but he couldn't. If he had to move his shoulder again, he was going to scream.

"You're bleeding," she whispered. "You're bleeding a lot."

Cavanaugh wasn't moving, but Cole wasn't sure for how long. He thought about standing up, but he was pretty sure that would do him in. Bryn was right, he was bleeding like a stuck pig.

"Get help," he said. "I'm not sure how long Cavanaugh's going to be out. And I'm not sure how long

I won't be. Get something to tie him up. The phone cord."

Bryn's face went completely white in the yellow lance of the oil lamp. She ran into the office and came back with the cord. She pushed Drake over and wrapped his wrists in the cord and tied it tightly with shaking fingers.

"I don't want to leave you here," she told him with frantic eyes. "Let's just go. I'll drive you to the hospital—"

"Get Brouchard. I'm not leaving Cavanaugh here alone and risk that he wakes up and gets away somehow. We'll leave Brouchard here with Cavanaugh then we'll go to the hospital and get the police." He just managed to keep her in focus. "Go get him now. Take the gun." He pushed it across the floor to her, the movement searing pain out from his shoulder, into his chest and all the way down his arm.

"Why?"

"Because if I pass out before you get back and he gets out of that cord, he's going to kill me with it."

She stared at him for an agonized beat. She took the gun in her trembling grip. "I'll be right back."

He grabbed her face, and it almost killed him. Darkness swam in front of his eyes. He connected with her worried, panicked gaze, let it hold him in the light. "I love you," he whispered. "Now go!" She blinked shock, tears filling her beautiful eyes. "Hurry!"

She pushed to her feet, flung open the door and disappeared into the storm.

Cavanaugh hadn't moved. Papers from that damn folder he'd carried were strewn everywhere. Agonized beats passed. Cole drew all his strength together, gritted his teeth and reached for the nearest one.

And he realized all the mistakes he'd made before were nothing compared to the one he'd made now.

Chapter 18

The night was a violent stew around her. Rain and wind buffeted her as she ran for her life, for Cole's life. She pounded her fist against Emile Brouchard's door, heart thundering.

"Does your phone work?" she gasped when he opened it. His cottage was dark except for a kerosene lantern in the corner. His old eyes took in her drenched form.

"It's dead," he said. "The storm."

"Oh, God." She'd been hoping, praying. Lightning slashed down again and she shivered under the porch overhang of the cottage. Beyond, she could see her mother's cottage was dark except for a tiny flickering light in the front window, probably a candle. Her electricity would be out, too, and her phone as well. It wasn't just the line to the mansion. It must have been a main line on the road that had gone down.

She grabbed Mr. Brouchard's arm. "Cole's been shot. Drake Cavanaugh came to the mansion tonight. I can't explain everything right now, but I need you to come with me. Now."

"You're not making sense, Miss Louvel." He didn't budge. "Are you all right? What are you doing with a gun?" He grabbed her arm with his free one and shook her slightly as if he thought she were hysterical.

Urgency pummeled in her veins. She wanted to run back to Cole, but Emile had her arm in a tight clamp. He was looking at her as if he was sure she'd lost her mind, and she was sure she sounded like she had.

"I'm fine!" she cried. "This is Drake's gun. I told you, he shot Cole. We have to get help. I'll drive into town with Cole. You have to stay with Drake until the police get here. Take the gun. In case he wakes up." She shoved the small, heavy weapon into his chest and he let go of her to take it. She didn't know how to use it anyway and she was relieved to get rid of it.

She turned to run but he grabbed her arm again. "You've got to tell me what this is about, Miss Louvel."

"There's not time. Let's just go."

"Tell me why Cavanaugh shot Dempsey."

She wanted to scream. "I don't have time to explain!" But he still wasn't letting go of her. "Drake came to the house tonight with some papers he found in his father's things," she blurted in a rush. "He was there, the night Aimee died. Hugh Cavanaugh thought Drake killed Aimee. He'd struggled with Aimee and she'd scratched his face. His father knew Drake's DNA was there and Drake would look guilty. Maybe he did kill Aimee, I don't know. Please, let's go."

But still he held onto her arm. "Tell me why he came to the house tonight."

Bryn blew out a frustrated breath. "His father and Randol Ormond and Frank Skelly got rid of the DNA. But Cole got the original forensic document from Ormond, before it was altered. We're having Aimee's body exhumed. Skelly's going to talk. Drake demanded the forensic report, the original, and he'd give us what was in that folder."

"Where is it?" Mr. Brouchard demanded. "The original?"

"I don't know! He's crazy. He shot Cole. He's still there, Mr. Brouchard. Cole knocked him out, but I don't know for how long. Cole's bleeding, badly. He needs help. Let's go."

"What was in the folder?"

"I don't know. Something about proof that my mother had an affair. Some papers Drake found in his father's things. I don't care. We have to go." She pulled away from him. "Please."

She turned away from the door to run back to the mansion. She had to get back to Cole before he—

The force of a blow sent her flying. She felt the shocking jolt of pain, then the blackness engulfed her.

"I wish you hadn't made me do this to you, Miss Louvel."

Bryn had trouble focusing as she opened her eyes. Her head pounded with an agonizing rhythm. Everywhere. Her head hurt everywhere. She heard a voice, but the words were lost in her brain.

"First Aimee, now you."

Aimee. Aimee's name broke through the mush of her head. Oh, God. The whirling cloud of her vision cleared. Her mouth felt thick, her tongue heavy.

Emile Brouchard stood over her.

A blast of fear spun through her blood. He'd hit her with something hard. Emile Brouchard had hit her, then she'd blacked out. And now—

Cole. She had to get to Cole.

Her vision swam as she moved her head. Somehow she had ended up on the floor of Emile Brouchard's cottage. And he was standing over her with Drake's gun. And it was pointed at her.

"If you move, I'll shoot you," he said quietly, calmly, as though it was no big deal. "And I really don't want to do that here."

"Mr. Brouchard—" Her voice came out in a scraping whisper. The mist closed in again and she fought it back. "Why?" was all she could manage.

"Let sleeping dogs lie, isn't that what they say,

Miss Louvel? But you couldn't do that, could you? You and Dempsey."

Emile Brouchard's short white hair tufted around his head as he peered down at her. The gun never moved from its position directed straight at her heart. Pain shivered through her. Mr. Brouchard looked like a giant angel leaning toward her…with the frigid, pale eyes of a demon.

"I don't like it when I have to kill people I care about," he continued in that oddly calm voice. "I didn't want to kill Aimee, but I had no choice. I really didn't want to kill Mathilde, but she was going to crack. She was going to go to the police. She was upset about Cole Dempsey asking questions. She was scared."

He'd killed Aimee. And he'd killed Mathilde. His own sister. Her head spun.

"I was real upset about that accident," Brouchard went on. "I didn't want to kill you when I cut those brake lines. It was supposed to be Dempsey."

Fear and panic gripped her. Now he was going to kill her. She had to escape, but she had no idea how. Her head felt as if it was going to explode every time she so much as moved it. And that gun was still pointed at her heart.

"I'm just glad my Patsy won't know this time. She grieved Aimee something fierce. She'll forget about you. She already has forgotten about you, hasn't she? She remembers me. Me and our Camellia."

Flowers. He was talking about flowers? And he was calling her mother *his Patsy*. Her mind stumbled to make sense of his words even as her focus wavered. Pain radiated from her crown to her toes.

"What are you talking about?" she whispered. She had to keep him talking. When he was done talking, he was going to kill her.

"Our baby," he said, and something fierce entered his voice. "Our baby Camellia."

His baby?

"What baby?"

"Foolish girl." Now his tone turned harsh. His eyes peering over her burned like liquid mercury. "You didn't notice anything that was going on that summer, did you? Always sneaking off with that Dempsey boy. If Aimee hadn't noticed things, either, she wouldn't have had to die."

"Why did Aimee have to die?" Bryn asked, her voice hitching.

"She knew about the baby. She knew it was mine. She came up to Patsy's room that afternoon with her tea. She caught me with your mother."

Bryn's breath caught, and her heart tripped dully.

"Oh, Mathilde, she knew all along. She helped us. She covered up for us. But she was off that day and that stupid sister of yours brought the tea up before I was gone. Patsy said she'd take care of it, but Aimee was crying. I knew she'd be trouble."

"You were having an affair with my mother?"

They'd had a baby? A maelstrom of emotions tumbled through her. But she didn't understand. "Why did you kill Aimee?"

"Mr. Louvel, he fired Wade Dempsey. Patsy told him she was having an affair with him. She hadn't been feeling well, and when she'd gone to the doctor, a blood test proved she was in fact pregnant. She'd taken a test and when the doctor called, he told Mr. Louvel it was positive. It was that idiot Dr. Biddle. He was a friend of your father's. Biddle didn't know it wasn't Mr. Louvel's baby—couldn't be his baby because Patsy hadn't slept with him in years. But she protected me. I knew she would. She needed me. Mr. Louvel, all he cared about was his business. I was there for Patsy. I grew her camellias and I brought them to her. I paid attention to her. That's all she wanted, a little attention. And I gave her a lot of it."

Her mother. Her desperate, depressed mother who'd just wanted attention. Bryn felt sick as Emile Brouchard's words pounded painfully through her brain.

"Did she know?" she whispered roughly. God, don't let him say her mother knew—

"She thought Wade Dempsey killed Aimee," Mr. Brouchard said. "I went back that night. I heard Mr. Louvel order Wade Dempsey off the plantation. I heard them fighting, heard Dempsey threaten him before he left. And I waited. I wanted to see Patsy, make sure she was all right. But she drove off and Mr. Louvel chased after her."

The memories of that awful night slashed through Bryn's pain. There was so much she hadn't known then, and it was so much worse than she could have imagined.

"I saw you take off with that Dempsey boy. Aimee was outside, and Drake Cavanaugh came. They argued. I don't know about what, but when he left, I had my chance. I'd heard her tell you before you went down to the river that she was going to fix everything, that Wade Dempsey wouldn't be fired when she was through. And when she saw me, she told me what she was going to do. She was going to tell her father that it wasn't Wade Dempsey that Patsy had been sleeping with. It was me. She was going to fix everything— for you, so you could keep whoring around with that piece-of-scum Dempsey boy."

Oh God, oh God. Guilt burned through her chest. Aimee had died because of her. Aimee had been determined to fix everything—for her.

"She knew about the baby. She'd heard me and Patsy talking about it when she came in the room."

Then Aimee had gone into town and met with Erica Saville and asked questions about pregnancy. Now it all fit. The puzzle pieces clicked in place. But it was too late.

"It would have ruined everything if Aimee had told the truth," he explained simply. "I had no choice. I had to kill her. I had to do it for Patsy and for me. I couldn't leave my Patsy. And Patsy wouldn't come away with me. She wouldn't leave you and Aimee. She knew Mr. Louvel had the power to keep you girls if she divorced him."

He said it as if it were all perfectly rational. He hadn't had a choice. He'd done what he had to do to stay with Patsy. Even if that meant killing one of her girls.

"Wade Dempsey came back drunk," he went on calmly. "He saw me with Aimee. She wasn't dead yet. I'd hit her and she'd fallen down. I'd knocked the wind out of her, that's all. We fought, Dempsey and I, and then I heard the cars coming up the drive. Aimee screamed and I shoved her down again. She hit her head and I knew she was dead that time. By the time Mr. Louvel got there, I was gone and he wasn't listening to anything Dempsey had to say. He was too drunk to talk straight anyway. He shot him dead. Good riddance," he spat.

Bryn felt cold nausea wash her. She had to keep him talking.

"What happened to the baby?"

"Patsy went to the sanitarium. She got Hugh Cavanaugh to draw up adoption papers for her. She called me and told me about it. She knew Mr. Louvel wasn't going to let her keep the baby, and I just wanted her to come back. She told me she was going to name her Camellia if it was a girl. She had a couple in the Midwest who was going to take her and they'd promised to keep the name. I just wanted her to come home, to come back to me. I knew she still wouldn't leave Bellefleur. She wouldn't leave you.

"She'd lost enough. She still had you, she still had me, and I had her. She moved into the cottage. She's happy. I make her happy."

And she always kept a camellia with her bone china angels. Bryn's heart clenched.

"What happened to Camellia?" she breathed.

"She was stillborn. And by then, it was all over. Cavanaugh, I don't think he was sure if it was Wade Dempsey or his own damn son who'd killed Aimee, but he wasn't going to risk anything. They covered it up, Cavanaugh and Ormond and Skelly. Nobody could bring back Aimee and nobody wanted to know who killed her anyway. Nobody but you and that damn Cole Dempsey. Fifteen years later. Now you dig up the past. Well, now you'll find out what happens when you don't let sleeping dogs lie."

"Drake thought Wade Dempsey was the father of my mother's baby," Bryn said suddenly, sharply. Her fogged mind struggled for clarity. "He had to. He brought that folder to me and Cole. He said it was proof my mother had slept with Wade Dempsey and he was going to tell everyone if we didn't give him the original forensic report."

"Hugh Cavanaugh and Mr. Louvel didn't know what I knew—that Wade Dempsey was sterile," Mr. Brouchard hissed. "If anyone sees those papers now, they're going to start asking questions. There's no way Mr. Louvel would have put his own child up for adoption, and I'm not the only one who knew Wade Dempsey couldn't have been the father of that baby. They're going to wonder who else could have been the father."

"But they won't be asking questions if you and Drake and Dempsey are dead. Once I'm through with you," he said, menacing over her. "I'll take care of Cavanaugh and Dempsey. Nobody ever has to know about the baby, and nobody will care who killed Aimee. They'll shut down the investigation. You, Dempsey, Cavanaugh. You're all about to meet an unfortunate end. When I cut the phone lines at the great house, I figured it would just be over for you and Dempsey. But all three of you together is even better. Get up. Now!"

"They'll care who killed me," Bryn gasped, horror soaking her. "They'll care who killed Drake and Cole."

"I'll make it look like Cavanaugh did it. It's his gun, isn't it? He shot Cole—and if I have to, I'll shoot him again. I'll make sure he's dead. And you." His eyes fired deadly resolve. "Then Cavanaugh turned the gun on himself. You'll all be dead."

Bryn's heart screamed for Cole. She was going to die and so was he if Mr. Brouchard took her back to the house. Cole was bleeding horribly, might be unconscious already.

A gunshot ripped past her ear, into the floor. "Get up," Brouchard ordered.

She tasted panic and pain. She scrambled to her feet. Her vision swam again and she nearly blacked out. But she couldn't pass out. She had to get away. He was going to take her back to Bellefleur. She had to escape.

He waved the gun at her and she stumbled to the door. She yanked it open. She could do this. She could get away. She had no choice but to try.

She pulled open the door. He was right behind her. Rain spattered and the wind whipped. She stumbled off the porch and then she ran.

Pain blasted through her head again and the next thing she knew she was on the ground, black spots everywhere. Mr. Brouchard jammed the gun against her neck.

"Don't try that again," he rasped. He jerked her to her feet and he pushed her forward. She could barely see. She tasted blood and her head roared.

It seemed like forever, but it could only have been minutes. He pushed her up the portico steps of Bellefleur. The door lay open. In the spill of the oil lamp, Drake's body hadn't moved. His eyes weren't open.

A bloody smear was all that was left of Cole. He was gone. Hope unfurled in her chest but she had no time to wonder where he'd gone.

The butt end of the pistol connected with the back of her head. She slammed onto the floor, pain ricocheting through her body. A gunshot blasted, and oil and fire spattered everywhere. With a shock, she realized he'd shot out the lamp. Twisting desperately, she found the gun pointed at her. He was going to kill them all—and leave Bellefleur on fire!

A solid shape appeared from the doorway into the office. A dark, hulking bloodied creature swam through Bryn's shocked vision.

Cole lunged forward, sank something dark and heavy on the back of Brouchard's head. Emile crumpled as oil from the lamp spread across the floor, igniting flames that rushed up the drapes as they reached the windows. Bryn felt the blackness swamping her again, but she pushed her eyes open by sheer will. They had to get out. And Cole looked as though he was about to collapse.

"This place is going to go up fast. I can't carry you, sweetheart. I can barely carry myself." Whatever adrenaline had brought him this far, he was fading fast. His face was white in the shining fire.

Bryn reeled to her feet. In another few seconds, the flames were going to consume the foyer. Then she saw he wasn't leaving. Unsteady as he was, he was going back for Drake, and she knew he'd never do it alone. He'd collapse. And she wasn't leaving Cole, not again.

"Get out," he yelled at her, but she reached down with numbed fingers to help him drag Drake's heavy, unconscious body. They made it onto the portico, stumbling down the steps where they left Drake. Blood soaked Cole's shirt and the blackness closed in on her vision as they fell helplessly to the wet ground.

Bellefleur was burning. The aching, anguished thought roiled through the mists of her pain-seared mind.

She floated, cold, in the hot, wet night. Crackling fire spat somewhere nearby, and she knew she had to open her eyes, had to move. Had to go back for Mr. Brouchard. Had to try to put out the fire.

Her legs collapsed under her when she tried to stand, and she sank, heartsick and nauseous, to the sodden ground. It was too late for Bellefleur, too late for Emile Brouchard. The foyer was ablaze and already it had gone through to the second story. Fire spat from an upper window. Rain poured down onto her face, but inside, the flames roared.

Indigo sky lit by sparks rolled above her, and she swung her hurting gaze to the man at her side. The completely still, bleeding man she loved.

"Cole," she whispered, pleaded, leaning over him to clutch his dear face as the nightmare of fire and rain raged on. He'd lost so much blood. Panicked fingers tore through her, clamping tight to her heart. "I love you. Don't die on me. I need you."

He opened his eyes, his beautiful, intense, searing eyes. Far, far in the distance, she heard sirens. From her mother's cottage, Emmie burst onto the path toward them.

Help was coming. Finally.

"Bryn—"

"Shhh. Don't talk. "

"No, but…Cavanaugh…the adoption papers—"

"I know. I know everything. Your father's innocent. It's over, " she said, and she started crying.

"No." He reached up a shaking, desperate, hopeful hand to touch her face. "It's just begun. I need you, too. I love you."

And if he was all she had left, she knew then and there he was more than enough. He was everything.

He always had been.

Epilogue

The healing—both physical and emotional—came in slow degrees, one day at a time. Cole saw it as a journey, a path to the future. His life had become more than his past.

They found Mathilde's body in the garden where Emile Brouchard had been digging. The investigation into Aimee's murder had gone wild in the press as Skelly and Cavanaugh traded confessions and barbs, blaming each other and Ormond and anyone else they could find to point a finger at. Brouchard had died in the fire that had burned Bellefleur, and Patsy Louvel had been no more than vaguely cognizant of the events that had transpired or her role in them. As the tangle of secrets and lies came out, Harlan Michel got his wish—he became a star in the blitz of media coverage.

Cole couldn't have cared less. He managed to keep himself and Bryn out of the spotlight as much as possible. They'd found all the truth they needed in each other. In the ashes of the past, they'd discovered the future.

And Cole looked forward to every second of it more than he could have ever imagined, in a place he'd never dreamed he could be happy.

"It's coming along," Bryn said then, linking her fingers through his as they stood in the gauzy autumn evening and surveyed the day's progress at Bellefleur.

The mansion hadn't completely burned down—the rain had helped. There had been a shell worth recovering, rebuilding.

"Maybe by spring," he said softly, squeezing her hand. He felt the band of gold on her ring finger that he'd placed there a month after the fire. Two months since then and he still couldn't believe she was his wife. The joy of it filled all the empty, grieving places in his heart, leaving no room for the pain and bitterness that had once ruled him.

Bryn had found her own peace, too, even with Patsy. It was too late for her mother to understand the full consequences of her deceptions—and too late for Bryn to blame her. Like Cole, she was ready to move on. And somehow, in rebuilding Bellefleur, they'd also brought their two worlds together and made it theirs. The house would never be the same. And that was a good thing. It would be what they made it—a home.

For now they'd begun their life together in Baton Rouge, and Cole was back at work at his firm. But like Bryn, he couldn't walk away from Bellefleur now, not permanently, and Baton Rouge wasn't too far away for a commute. They'd have children someday. Children who deserved to know their legacy.

"What do you think of Alexandre?" she asked, looking up at him with amazing, clear water hyacinth eyes, no longer aching with hurt but shining instead with love.

Cole tugged his brows together. "Alexandre Louvel?" he guessed, trying to figure what she meant. "He saved our lives, that's what I think of him." It had been that small, heavy bust of the man who'd shaped Bellefleur's prosperity in the sugarcane business that he'd crashed down onto the back of Emile Brouchard's head that shocking night three months before. Alexandre Louvel had secured his family's future all over again.

Bryn's lips curved into a beautiful smile. "For the baby, silly. If it's a boy."

The oaks sighed as the breeze kicked up around them. Far away over the river, a brown pelican lifted up off the bank and soared.

Cole's heart burst. Understanding hit him, along

with an incredible sense of completeness. He claimed his wife's precious mouth in a hungry kiss. He would never get enough of Bryn, never. And now—

"Alexandre Dempsey," he breathed as he released her sweet mouth. "It sounds perfect to me."

And it was.

* * * * *

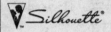

If you enjoyed what you just read,
then we've got an offer you can't resist!

Take 2 bestselling love stories FREE!

Plus get a FREE surprise gift!